"Dominic, what's happening?"

Cathy swallowed hard at the sudden tension between them.

"Does it really matter?" He was standing in front of her now.

It mattered more than anything else ever had in her life. But the situation was fast whirling out of control—the burning passion ignited between them as soon as their lips met.

She wrenched her mouth away from his, breathing hard. "What are you doing?" she gasped.

His lips traveled down the column of her throat. "I know it's been a long time for me," he murmured gruffly, "but I didn't think I was that out of practice."

She didn't care how long ago it was since he'd held a woman like this; the fact was, he was holding her now....

CAROLE MORTIMER, one of our most popular—and prolific—English authors, began writing in the Harlequin Presents series in 1979. She now has more than forty top-selling romances to her credit and shows no signs whatever of running out of plot ideas. She writes strong traditional romances with a distinctly modern appeal, and her winning way with characters and romantic plot twists has earned her an enthusiastic audience worldwide.

Books by Carole Mortimer

Don't miss any of our special offers. Write to us at the following address for information on our newest releases.

Harlequin Reader Service
901 Fuhrmann Blvd., P.O. Box 1397, Buffalo, NY 14240
Canadian address: P.O. Box 603,
Fort Erie, Ont. L2A 5X3

CAROLE MORTIMER

a christmas affair

Harlequin Books

TORONTO • NEW YORK • LONDON
AMSTERDAM • PARIS • SYDNEY • HAMBURG
STOCKHOLM • ATHENS • TOKYO • MILAN

For
Frank
With Love

Harlequin Presents first edition December 1990
ISBN 0-373-11325-0

Original hardcover edition published in 1990
by Mills & Boon Limited

CHAPTER ONE

WHAT were you supposed to do when the man you were in love with didn't even seem to realise you were female, let alone that you had lustful feelings towards him?

Cathy knew exactly what she was going to do, and Dominic Reynolds wasn't going to like it one little bit!

Even as the thought entered her mind—with a determination that was unshakeable—a bellow of rage came from within the adjoining office, quickly followed by the man himself exploding out of the room to cross to her desk with forceful strides.

Mary, one of the secretaries from the outer office, had been in the middle of a conversation with Cathy, but she took one look at Dominic's thunderous expression and scuttled from the room.

Cathy's own manner was as casual as usual as she continued to look through the papers strewn across her desktop, shaking her head derisively. 'If Mary wasn't of a nervous disposition before she came to work for you, she certainly is now,' she drawled in an amused voice, not at all perturbed herself by his obvious bad temper—or the reason for it.

Dominic scowled. 'I don't give a damn about Mary's nerves.'

'That's the trouble with you,' Cathy bit out tautly, her eyes flashing with anger, coloured a deep smoky grey by the emotion. 'You "don't give a damn" about anyone else's feelings but your own!'

Dominic's mouth tightened: a finely chiselled mouth that looked too perfect to firm with temper or thin with displeasure—and yet Cathy knew it was capable of much worse than that; Mary hadn't got her nervous disposition for no reason during the last three months she had worked as one of Dominic's secretaries.

'What the hell do you call this?' He waved a piece of headed paper in front of her nose.

Cathy didn't flinch, coolly raising blonde brows at the object that so offended him. 'Well,' she said with a casual lack of interest, 'I don't know what you call it, but it looks decidedly like a letter to me.' She looked at him challengingly.

His harshly indrawn breath showed he wasn't in the least amused by her levity at his expense. But at this precise moment Cathy didn't particularly care what he felt. Maybe she would later—she was sure she would later!—but right now she was only concerned with showing him *she* didn't give a damn.

Which was a complete fabrication. She had cared about Dominic from that very first interview with him five years ago, had loved him almost from the day she came to work for him. But, as she very well knew, Dominic didn't care about anyone or anything, only about being successful—which, with his varied and profitable enterprises, he certainly was.

Women were a non-event in his life, Dominic not even seeming to see them most of the time. Which Cathy had found, when she had been told on more than one occasion that she was beautiful enough to be a model, could be very frustrating.

Perhaps if she didn't love him, if Dominic didn't look like a romantic hero himself, with his slightly overlong dark hair, fierce green eyes, perfectly chiselled features, and tall, muscular body invariably clothed in a three-piece suit of one sombre colour or another, it wouldn't have mattered quite so much what he thought—or rather, didn't think—of women.

But Dominic had the sort of male good looks that could stop conversation in a room when he entered it, could have—and had had!—an Arabian princess promising him half her father's kingdom if he would marry her. The former he seemed genuinely not to notice, and

the latter he had ignored as a childish prank—
except that Cathy knew the princess had been
perfectly in earnest!

But what could you do with a man who had
never, to Cathy's knowledge, even invited a
woman out with him for the evening during the
whole time she had worked for him?

To Dominic, social occasions were just an
extension of work, and if he required a female
companion for one of those occasions then
Cathy, as his personal assistant, would do.

He could be so flattering to a woman's ego!

And sarcasm wasn't going to get her anywhere, she acknowledged miserably.

Nothing she had done the last five years had
got her anywhere with this man; to him she
was just a second storage unit for all his
business dealings, his right-hand man, his Man
Friday. She might just as well have *been* a man
for all the notice he took of her.

Which brought her right back to the reason
for his fury with her now.

'You demanded to have time off for
Christmas even though you knew it wasn't
convenient,' he rasped, his eyes glittering
angrily. 'You even persuaded me into letting
you use the Audi Quattro when you suddenly
decided you had to leave for your sister's home
in Devon in the middle of the night while a
snowstorm raged. And then,' he breathed

deeply, 'after only one night away instead of the week you had insisted upon, you arrived back here to give me this!' He slapped the letter angrily against the palm of his other hand.

'Let's just get the facts straight, shall we?' She straightened, her gaze unflinching—one thing: no matter how arrogantly demanding he was, he had never managed to fray her nerves to breaking-point as he had poor Mary and the other secretaries. And he wasn't about to start now! 'It's never convenient with you if I take a holiday, let alone want to spend Christmas with my family. Just because you don't believe in them—families *or* Christmas—there's no reason to think that the rest of the world isn't entitled to them either!'

His jaw was clenched tightly at her verbal blows. 'I don't think the rest of the world——'

'All right, then, maybe it's just my wanting a holiday with my family that you find so offensive,' she snapped irritably.

'You took your damned holiday, two days early, no matter what my feelings were,' he scowled. 'So what's the problem?'

'I haven't got to that yet,' she grated, eyes narrowed angrily. 'Secondly,' she said pointedly, 'I did not persuade you into letting me take the Audi, you *offered*. Thirdly,' she continued determinedly as he would have interrupted, 'I went to my sister's so suddenly *not* because of some trivial female whim, which is what you seem to be implying, but because of an emergency!'

'An emergency that is obviously over now, or you wouldn't be back here,' said Dominic impatiently. 'So I still don't see what the problem is.'

Oh, yes, the emergency was definitely over now. Cathy smiled to herself as she thought of the ecstatic telephone call she had received from her friend Jade late the previous evening telling her of the wedding she and David were planning for the New Year. It could so easily have worked out unhappily for all concerned.

But the joy Jade and David had undoubtedly found in each other had only strengthened her own resolve where Dominic was concerned, which was why she had come into the office at all today.

'Fourthly,' she told him firmly, 'I gave you that——' she indicated the letter he crushed so savagely in his hand '—because I no longer want to work for you.'

He drew in a harsh breath. 'Just like that?' He was outraged.

No, not just like that. She no more wanted to leave than he seemed to want her to go. But their reasons for that were completely different. She because just being close to him had to be better than nothing; he because, as they both knew, he didn't want to lose the best personal assistant he had ever had.

But, after five years of believing that being close to him was better than nothing, Cathy knew that was no longer true. She loved him, would always love him, but she was twenty-six, and if she wanted to make any sort of life for herself she knew she would have to make the break now. Had known it, and had difficulty accepting it, for some time.

She shrugged non-committally, continuing to pack the things from the top of her desk into the box in front of her. 'After five years I think it's time for a change.'

'To do what?' he said with angry scorn, crushing even more the letter of resignation that had been the start of his fury.

'Maybe I'll take up modelling,' she shrugged after a moment's thought. 'Everyone seems to believe I have the face and figure for it.'

'You would be bored out of your mind within a week!' Dominic dismissed harshly, making no comment about what 'everyone believed' concerning her looks.

'As long as that?' she returned consideringly, her head tilted to one side, her hair blonde and silkily straight to her shoulders. 'Maybe I should give an agency a ring.'

'Cathy——'

'Yes, Dominic?' she prompted smoothly, knowing that her own coolness in the face of his agitation was adding to his frustration with a situation that seemed out of his control; Dominic liked to be in control at all times.

He glowered at her. 'If there's some sort of problem between us, couldn't you at least have come to me and talked about it instead of just leaving this on my desk for me to find when I went through my mail?' Once again he slapped the crumpled paper against the palm of his hand.

'But there is no problem,' she told him dismissively. 'And where else would you have liked me to leave my letter of resignation? It wouldn't have done a lot of good sitting on *my* desk, now, would it?' she chided reasoningly.

His eyes narrowed warningly at her continued flippancy. 'I would rather you hadn't left the damned thing anywhere.'

'But then you wouldn't have known I was leaving,' she pointed out practically, picking up the calendar from the side of her desk, debating whether or not it belonged to her personally or to the office, and finally throwing it carelessly into the top of her box.

'Will you stop being so damned—uncaring?' Dominic exploded once again.

This volatile temper, joined by his razor-sharp brain, was something the City knew to be very wary of.

To Cathy, these occasional lapses of temper just showed he was human after all!

'Oh, lighten up, Dominic,' she advised him impatiently. ' "It's Christmas Eve, and all's right with the world," ' she quoted drily.

'Not *my* world,' he rasped. 'God, Cathy, no one gives immediate notice!'

She was aware of that; she also knew that her having done so, and insisting that it go through, could be serious enough to make Dominic refuse to give her a reference.

But she had made her decision to make the break and, having done so, she didn't want to be anywhere near Dominic, where her resolve could so easily be weakened, until she felt strong enough to cope with seeing him again. Maybe in a hundred years or so!

'We have a contract, Cathy,' he reminded her hardly. 'It states that there should be three months' notice on either side. If you go ahead with leaving immediately I could sue you for breach of that contract.'

She winced, knowing that if he got angry enough he was as likely to do just that. 'At Christmas?' She shook her head disgustedly. 'I always wondered what that middle initial "S" stood for in your name, and now I think I know: Scrooge could have taken lessons from you!'

Red colour stained his cheeks. 'I've always been fair with you——'

'Of course you have,' she cut in scornfully. 'That's why I've worked a constant sixty-hour week without holidays for the last five years!'

His mouth tightened. 'I always paid you for the extra hours.'

'Money isn't everything, Dominic,' she snapped scathingly. 'Oh, I'll admit I like the nice clothes and the apartment that money has allowed me to have, but at the rate I'm going I'll be too exhausted by the time I reach thirty to enjoy them any more! I'll just be a burnt-out money-grasper.'

'Like me, you mean?' He met her gaze challengingly, his eyes as hard as emeralds.

'Not at all,' she returned coolly. 'You'll never be burnt out; you thrive on this sort of life.' But they had both noticed, she was sure, that she made no comment on the second part of her description.

How much money did one man need? Dominic had far more money than one man could spend in a lifetime, in actual fact had no one to leave the money to when he was gone, so he didn't even have the excuse that he was doing it for his family. And yet he continued to work long hours, constantly pushing himself, and those around him, so that he could add more millions to those he already had.

Perhaps, if he actually seemed to go out and enjoy the money, Cathy could accept the way he was, but, apart from his luxurious apartment in town, his tailored clothes and his expensive cars, he spent very little on himself; not for him the playboy lifestyle his wealth could have afforded.

Not that Cathy relished the idea of his behaving in that cavalier fashion, but the way he forged forward, earning more and more money just to put it away and more or less forget about it, seemed to her to stem more from a compulsion than from any real enjoyment in the act, or in wealth itself.

His mouth twisted. 'But apparently it no longer appeals to you?'

'No,' she confirmed flatly.

He looked for a moment as if he would like to do her some sort of physical violence, although as usual he managed to keep himself under control.

'Even so,' he bit out, 'you must see that you have to honour the three months' notice in the contract you signed when you first came to work for me.'

Her brows quirked. 'The same way you've honoured the weeks' holidays I was supposed to have had each year, stated in that very same contract?' she reminded him without malice. 'I'll tell you what, Dominic, you forget about the three months' notice you say I owe you, and I'll forget all those weeks' holiday you owe me. And you'll still come out very much a winner!'

His expression was grim as he looked down into her calm but determined face. 'I'm beginning to realise I made a mistake in working you so hard all these years,' he said slowly. 'You're obviously very much in need of a holiday; you seem to be suffering from a form of nervous exhaustion.'

'Because I handed in my resignation?' She smiled, her expression pitying. 'You really don't know me very well at all, do you, Dominic?' she added with sad stoicism.

'Of course I know you, damn it,' he rasped. 'I've spent almost every waking moment with you for the last five years!'

More than a lot of married couples, in fact, and yet Cathy knew she was still far from knowing the real man that was Dominic. Oh, she knew the basic things, such as his liking for black coffee for breakfast, the way he always wore black shoes, the fact that he liked to read *The Times* no matter what part of the world they happened to be in at the time; she was very familiar with all of his likes and dislikes in food, knew that he hated the farce of situation comedies on the television, that opera actually put him to sleep no matter whom he happened to be spending the evening with; and she also knew that alcohol was something he rarely indulged in. On a day-to-day basis she probably knew as much, if not more, than the average wife who'd known her husband the same number of years. And yet Dominic's real emotions he kept very low-key, and his past life was a closed book.

Dominic knew about her in just as much detail, but he was also privileged with the information that she had a sister called Penny with a family in Devon; he also knew about her life before the two of them had met and she had come to work for him.

As for her emotions, he didn't want to know about them!

'So you have,' she accepted lightly. 'Then you should know me well enough by now to realise that I haven't resigned lightly, without giving the whole thing serious thought.'

'Of course I realise that,' he grated tautly. 'Which is why I think it would be a good idea if you took the next week off, after all—two weeks, if you would prefer,' he amended hastily at her derisive expression. 'Take the time to rest yourself, to rethink your decision.'

'Two whole weeks, Dominic?' Cathy taunted. 'Are you sure you can spare them?'

'It has to be better than having you leave for good,' he rasped irritably.

Once again she smiled. 'Two weeks wouldn't be long enough.' She shook her head.

'Then take three weeks, a month. Damn it, Cathy,' he scowled. 'Talk to me!'

Now he wanted to talk to her. Although she didn't delude herself into thinking he wanted to talk about anything other than persuading her into continuing to work for him.

'My letter of resignation says it all, Dominic.' She shrugged dismissively, looking through the drawers in her desk to see if there was anything she had forgotten, before moving across the room to the window-ledge where she had slowly nurtured plants over the years into healthy adult plants; to leave them behind now would be like leaving part of herself behind. And she intended no part of her to remain here once she had physically left.

Dominic followed her, and although Cathy didn't acknowledge his presence next to her as she filled the box with the plants, she could feel his nervous energy.

'You say you want to move on to something different,' he quoted impatiently. 'But why? You know you love this job!'

The statement had nothing to do with egotism; she had never made any secret of her enjoyment of the work she did for Dominic, which she had loved from the very first moment, and she would only be fooling herself if she didn't admit she was going to miss the constant excitement the work involved. But her ragged and bruised emotions knew best, realised when it was time to admit defeat in the face of indifference, and move on. Which was exactly what she intended doing.

Besides—and this was something Dominic would never understand—it had never been just a job to her; it had been the only sort of partnership she could ever have with him.

'So I'll learn to love a new job,' she told him with confident bravado, looking out of the window at the greying sky. 'It looks full of snow,' she murmured to herself.

'You were born to be my personal assistant,' Dominic said frustratedly in the face of her obviously wandering attention. 'Maybe some shares in DomRey would give you more of an incentive to reconsider.' His eyes were narrowed to emerald slits.

She laughed softly at the suggestion. 'You don't need a partner, Dominic.'

'I wasn't offering partnership,' he snapped. 'Just the interest of a few shares in the company you work for.'

'Thanks, but no, thanks,' she refused without the slightest hesitation, glancing up at the sky again; if only it didn't look that awful white-grey colour that often preceded snow! 'Just hold off another five or six hours,' she requested of it pleadingly, turning with the box in her arms to knock Dominic full in the chest where he stood so close to her. 'Sorry,' she grimaced, stepping aside to make sure she missed him this time.

'But those shares you've just turned down are worth over—— '

'I *am* a good PA, Dominic,' she said without turning. 'I know what they're worth.'

'Then——'

'I'm not interested, in them or in their worth,' she stated firmly, glancing worriedly at her watch; the day was quickly moving on, and she still had a lot to do.

'Am I keeping you?' Dominic demanded irritably as he saw that glance.

Cathy looked up at him, answering him calmly, 'As a matter of fact, yes.'

'I'm so sor—good God!' Sarcasm gave way to alarm as he once again followed her across the room. 'Those mutterings about snow and hoping it will hold off for five or six hours don't mean that you're thinking of driving back down to Devon today, do they?' He looked disbelieving.

Considering that she had driven down through the night two days ago, and then back again yesterday evening, Dominic could be forgiven for looking at her as if she must have taken leave of her senses. But she had had very good reasons for making both those unscheduled journeys, and if Dominic had ever shown the slightest interest in her personal life she might have been tempted to confide them to him.

As things had turned out she had more reason than ever for wanting to be back among her family for Christmas. She intended to be there with them all when Jade and David celebrated their engagement; those two, more than anyone else she knew, deserved happiness, and she was thrilled that they had found it together.

'And if it does?' she challenged.

'Then I no longer just *think* I've been working you too hard, I *know* I have,' he returned grimly. 'You must know as well as I do that the long-term weather forecast is snow, snow, and more snow. You would have to be insane to go out into that again!'

She raised blonde brows. 'I don't think I have to take that sort of talk from you now.'

Green eyes flashed. 'I'm just offering you sound common sense.'

'Dominic, you never *offer* advice,' she mocked lightly.

He stiffened, very tall and handsome in the navy blue three-piece suit. 'Meaning?'

'Meaning that I intend going back to Devon today, no matter what the weather forecast, no matter what you have to say about it——'

'No matter what anyone says, by your reckless attitude,' he bit out tersely. 'When did you get to be so damned stubborn?'

'Oh, I've always been pretty determined,' she dismissed casually. 'You've just never taken the time to notice before now.' As he hadn't noticed a lot of other things about her!

Like the very fact that she loved him madly, passionately—futilely.

There had never even been the faintest flicker of awareness on his part of her as a woman. It was all so—depressing.

But she wasn't about to let him see *that* emotion, today of all days. He might just misinterpret the reason behind that depression. Oh, she was upset at the thought of no longer working for him, but it was the thought of leaving Dominic as a person that was upsetting her more—the fact that her love for him had always gone by completely unrecognised by him.

Not that she wanted him to see her like some fawning idiot, either, with no hope of having him return her love. That was the trouble with loving Dominic; she couldn't ever come out the winner.

Which was why she had to go.

Now, before the flippant façade she had constructed over what she had just done cracked a mile wide and left her emotionally broken...

'Cathy——'

'I have to go, Dominic,' she told him lightly, doing her best to shut out that huskily persuasive voice; if Dominic chose to put his mind to it he could charm the birds out of the trees. He just didn't feel so inclined most of the time and, even when he did, impatience and temper usually took over.

'The snow isn't going to hold off forever,' she told him brightly, shaking back her hair as she picked up the box again in readiness for leaving. 'I guess I'll have to forgo the usual leaving party,' she added self-derisively; she had never envisaged leaving Dominic in quite these circumstances. She had never envisaged leaving him at all!

His expression darkened even more, almost black brows low over his eyes.

Cathy wished she hadn't looked at those eyes. They were incredibly beautiful eyes for a man, a deep emerald-green, surrounded by the thickest black lashes she had ever seen.

Oh, the dreams she had once had of one day holding a baby of her own in her arms with those eyes, Dominic's eyes...

She swayed slightly, her lids closed over the tears that had welled there. How foolish were her dreams!

'Damn the leaving party.' The rasp of Dominic's voice steadied her, and she met his gaze calmly. 'You're too tired to drive all that way again today; you're almost asleep on your feet!'

If she was honest, she *didn't* relish the journey for a third time in as many days, but there was no way she was going to miss being with the family for the festive season for the first time in years.

Where had she and Dominic spent Christmas last year? Oh, yes, in a hotel in New York, going over contracts that were finalised as soon as Christmas Day had passed. And the year before that they had been at another hotel, that time in Munich. And the year before that... Oh, what was the use of dwelling in the past? *This* Christmas she intended being surrounded by the warmth of her family, by people giving and receiving gifts in love and friendship.

She quickly banished from her mind the image she suddenly had of Dominic completely alone at his apartment, with no one to give him even one present and show him love. That was the way he *wanted* it, the way it always was.

'It's Christmas Eve,' she said again brightly. 'The thought of spending Christmas with the family will be enough to keep me awake and alert. Oh, I forgot to tell you——' her eyes glowed with pleasure '—David is there, too.'

Dominic frowned. 'You mean David Kendrick?'

'Mm.' She smiled confirmation. 'You knew my sister is married to his brother?'

'I believe you did tell me,' Dominic nodded abruptly. 'But I also thought he wasn't—into family occasions?'

'Oh, all that's changed,' Cathy laughed happily at the thought of how loving Jade had changed David's life. 'It promises to be a wonderful Christmas with all the family together again at last.'

Dominic thrust his hands into his trouser pockets, turning away to gaze out of the window at London's bleak skyline. 'Then I'd better not keep you any longer.'

It should have been her turn to say, 'Just like that?' No matter what she had said in the last few minutes, she couldn't believe this was really goodbye. But she knew that it had to be, and the uncompromising set of Dominic's shoulders beneath the tailored jacket didn't encourage her to say the actual words to him.

She took one last lingering look at the room and the man before rushing out of the door.

How she managed to say goodbye to Mary and the other secretaries in the outer office she didn't know; her throat was aching with the effort of holding back the tears by the time she got outside the building, and she almost fell inside the taxi she hailed.

And then the tears fell like a waterfall.

The driver shot her a worried glance in his driving-mirror. 'Christmas party?'

She would have laughed at the suggestion if she could have stopped feeling miserable long enough; the closest Dominic came to recognising Christmas was to let his staff leave an hour earlier than usual!

But she nodded anyway, because it was what the driver obviously expected to hear, and also because she was starting to cry again.

Thank God she had packed her case and done her few errands before going to the office this morning. Now she just wanted to get away, pausing only long enough to change into warm clothes for the journey ahead of her. The last thing she wanted was to be alone in her flat any longer than she had to be.

Which was why she muttered and mumbled to herself as the doorbell rang just as she was bending down to pick up her suitcase. It was probably the janitor calling for his Christmas tip!

She stared dazedly up at Dominic as he stood outside her door, no longer the suave executive in the formal suit, but looking just as devastatingly attractive in fitted black trousers and a thick Aran sweater worn beneath a black leather jacket.

Having resigned herself to the possibility of perhaps never seeing him again, Cathy could only stare at him in stunned surprise.

'As you're so adamant about going down to Devon again today,' he told her in measured tones, 'I've decided to drive you.'

CHAPTER TWO

CATHY forgot about how devastated she had been such a short time ago at the thought of not seeing Dominic again, completely forgot her joy of a few moments ago when she had opened her door and found him standing there, too.

All she could think of at the moment was his damned *typical* arrogance!

She made no effort to open her apartment door wider or invite him to come in. 'Isn't it usual to ask?' she snapped tautly, controlling her anger with great difficulty.

Dominic shrugged dismissively. 'I knew you never would.'

Her eyes widened incredulously. 'I wasn't talking about me!' she gasped.

His eyes narrowed, and he walked past her into the apartment with easy familiarity, despite Cathy's unwelcoming attitude. 'Why would I need to ask to drive you down to Devon?' he said with genuine amazement. 'I'm the one doing you a favour.'

Cathy had followed him agitatedly into the

elegantly furnished lounge. 'You can take your favour and——'

'I've already spoken to your brother-in-law, and he agrees with me——'

'You've telephoned Simon?' she gasped again, her eyes even wider than before.

Dominic gave an arrogant inclination of his head. 'Actually, during the course of the conversation he invited me to spend Christmas with you and the family,' he revealed distantly.

Simon would. Her brother-in-law was one of the kindest, most warm-hearted, most generous people she had ever known, and the thought of someone spending the festive season on their own would easily move him to make the invitation to Dominic. And he would have meant it sincerely, too.

Goodness knew, Dominic was far from being a stranger to Penny and Simon; even though the other couple had never actually met him, Cathy had talked about him often enough!

And she hadn't yet had an opportunity to tell Simon and her sister that she was no longer working for Dominic.

She eyed him warily across the room. 'And what was your answer?'

His mouth twisted mockingly. 'Don't worry, I don't willingly go where I know I'm not wanted.'

'Oh, but I'm sure Simon——'

'I wasn't talking about your brother-in-law,' he drawled dismissively.

Her cheeks burned with heated colour. 'It has nothing to do with me whom Simon chooses to invite into his home,' she told him stiltedly.

'Nevertheless,' Dominic's mouth firmed, 'despite your brother-in-law's kind invitation—which, incidentally, I'm sure was genuine—I have no intention of intruding upon the Christmas that means so much to you.'

Considering Dominic never acknowledged the festive season by so much as a sprig of holly in his office, Cathy couldn't imagine that he had ever seriously considered the invitation anyway! She certainly didn't feel as if she was depriving him of anything by being the real reason he had declined!

'All the more reason for you not to drive me down to Devon,' she dismissed.

'I don't have anything else to do.' He shrugged broad shoulders. 'And as we are both well aware——' his mouth twisted derisively '—the whole world grinds to a halt at Christmas.'

'That's never seemed to stop you before,' Cathy recalled drily.

He shrugged. 'This year I seem to be without my capable PA. And a few hours' notice isn't time enough for me to be able to train up another one,' he added hardily.

She didn't even blink at his sarcasm. 'I have no wish to talk about work.'

'Neither have I,' he drawled, glancing out of the window of her flat. 'Snow looks imminent, so if you want to leave...'

'I'll go when I'm ready.' She spoke with more stubbornness than good sense, because snow *did* look imminent.

'Strange.' Dominic looked at her consideringly, just as if he were viewing a somewhat wayward child in his presence. 'I never considered you a foolish person until today.'

Possibly because today was the first time he had seen her as even being halfway human, rather than just a business extension of himself!

'Stubborn *and* foolish,' she derided. 'What makes you think you're any more capable of driving to Devon than I am?' she challenged, her eyes glittering a dark smoky grey.

'I don't,' he surprised her by answering. 'But at least with the two of us there we could take it in turns to do the driving, and in that way we could halve the strain.'

Cathy hated it when he made good sense, especially when it was about something as important as this! How could she refuse his help now without looking absolutely stupid? Especially when she was well aware of the fact that she couldn't possibly be upsetting any of his own plans for Christmas; he had probably intended to hibernate until all the 'childish emotion', as she had once heard him describe it, was over.

'I'm still not prepared to talk about my resignation,' she told him firmly.

The grimness relaxed slightly about his mouth, as if he was well aware that a victory of one kind was imminent. 'I've already said I don't want to talk about it either. But if at some time during the journey you *should* decide you would like to discuss it——'

'I won't,' she insisted abruptly. 'It's a fact, irreversible, un——'

'I think I get the message, Cathy,' he drawled at her vehemence.

'In that case, what's in this for you?' She raised mocking brows.

'Nasty, Cathy,' he said. 'Very nasty.'

'Educated,' she corrected drily.

His mouth quirked in a facsimile of a smile. 'I trained you to be my right-hand man—you know me better than I know myself most of the time. And, knowing me as you do, you're right: I'm not going to give up hoping you'll change your mind.'

She knew he had invented the word 'tenacious'; she had always believed that that elusively unexplained 'S' in his initials stood for stubborn—no matter what she might earlier have accused to the contrary! And yet she had also never believed him capable of needing anyone, or anything, enough to put himself to the trouble of chasing after it. But maybe he considered the five years he had spent training her to be worth his making the exception!

She met his gaze challengingly. 'In that case, we had better get going, hadn't we?'

Dominic showed no surprise at her decision to accept his help after all, glancing across at her case and the wicker basket that stood ready in the hallway. 'Is that all you're taking with you?'

She might have realised he had known from the onset that he would have his own way! Arrogant, dictatorial, self-assured, pig-headed——! 'Yes,' she bit out tightly.

'Just a polite query,' he murmured tolerantly at her defensive attitude. 'No criticism intended.'

Cathy watched him with troubled eyes as he crossed the room to pick up her cases. Five to six hours alone in the confines of a car with him in the circumstances; she had to be insane.

She muttered to herself as she pulled her full-length dark green coat on over her black jumper and grey fitted trousers, preparing herself to follow him out of the flat.

God knew what this drive was going to be like, and yet in a strangely masochistic way she was actually looking forward to it!

He drove the Audi with an assurance Cathy couldn't hope to imitate when her own turn to drive came, long, tapered hands moving confidently on the wheel. And the snow was no longer imminent; it was falling gently on the road in front of them.

Dominic's attention was all grimly on what was on the other side of the car window, leaving *Cathy* free to gaze at him to her heart's content without fear of his noticing what she was doing. Just to look at him made her heart beat faster. His profile was so strong and handsome. He——

Dear lord, they weren't even out of London yet, and already she was in the middle of a hot flush over the man! She was going to be a physical wreck by the time they reached Devon!

Dominic had always had the power to affect her this way, but usually during the time they spent together she didn't have a moment to think, let alone allow her emotions for him to have free rein. But now there was no work to distract either of them . . .

'I never realised Christmas was important to you,' Dominic spoke suddenly in the strange stillness of late morning.

Cathy gave him a startled glance, sitting up straighter in her seat. 'You never asked.'

'More criticism?' He frowned darkly.

'Certainly not,' she answered truthfully. 'Why should an employer be interested in an employee's personal likes and dislikes?' And, as her pained heart knew, the two of them had certainly never crossed over that finely drawn line.

Dominic drew in a harsh breath. 'I thought we were at least—friends.'

Now it was Cathy's turn to frown. Dominic didn't have what she would have classed actual friends. He had a lot of acquaintances, but no one who was really close to him. And she had always believed he preferred it that way.

'Don't look so stunned, Cathy,' he drawled self-derisively. 'My obvious misapprehension doesn't bind you to anything.'

Friends? Dominic and she? If they were, it wasn't the sort of friendship she was used to— nothing at all like the friendship she had shared with Jade for so many years. With Jade, it didn't matter how long it had been since the two of them had last seen each other; they would instantly fall into a warm conversation as if it had been yesterday, talking about anything and nothing, whatever the two of them wished. She and Dominic had never talked like that together.

And yet she could see she had offended Dominic by her scepticism, and she wished there were some way she could undo her surprise at his assumption. It was the first time she had ever heard Dominic presume such a friendship existed between them, and now it looked as if she was throwing it back in his face!

'I've always hoped we were,' she returned non-committally.

But she had always believed that friends confided things to each other, and other than what she had read about Dominic's personal life in magazine articles, plus the few brief glimpses he had given her himself, she knew little or nothing about him.

And anyone could find out that he came from a working-class background, that his parents had died while he was relatively young, and that he had been brought up by a spinster aunt after that. She didn't need to read it anywhere to know that he never went out with women, or at least, if he did, he was very, very discreet. As regarded his business life, she knew all about that to the last detail. What she didn't know was what devil it was that drove him.

And if he really regarded her as a friend he would have felt able to confide at least part of the reason for his single-minded attitude to life.

But she only knew that he was the man she loved. At the same time, she knew that he had memories buried inside him, memories that had scarred too deeply for him to share them with anyone. She knew that instinctively, not from anything he had ever said or shown from his actions. There was evidence enough in the closed man that he was.

The times that she had hoped and prayed he would open up to her! But all he had ever chosen to discuss with her was business. That was never likely to change now. And it had obviously been enough for Dominic all these years.

'As close as I've got to having one,' he mockingly echoed her thoughts, as if he had found it all too easy to read them. He glanced at her. 'Why don't you settle down and have a sleep? And don't say you aren't tired,' he added softly as she went to protest. 'Because I know damn well you must be.'

'I was just about to remind you that you had agreed we would take it in turns to drive,' she said.

He shrugged. 'As we've only gone about fifteen miles, I think I might manage to carry on for a while longer!'

His sarcastic sense of humour had taken a lot of getting used to when she had first gone to work for him, especially as the closest he ever came to acknowledging that humour himself was the occasional glitter of amusement in the dark green eyes!

'I'll wake you when I've had enough,' he added drily.

She made a face at him, receiving a mocking quirk of his mouth in response. 'Just make sure you do,' she warned as she settled down more comfortably, closing her eyes.

'Yes, ma'am,' he drawled.

Cathy opened one eye and looked at him. 'Try and remember that in future I'm no longer restrained in my responses by the fact that I work for you,' she said.

'I can't say I ever noticed that fact keeping you silent in the past,' he mocked. 'Your honesty, brutal or otherwise, has always been one of the things I've most liked about you.'

She had never even realised he *did* like her. He had picked a hell of a time to decide to tell her he did!

Not that it would have made any difference to her earlier decision. Liking wasn't loving, and she was no longer willing to settle for anything less, especially the scraps Dominic was able to give her. Lord knew she had flared up at Jade about appreciating the value of love when it was offered to her; she couldn't then opt for anything less for herself.

She had a feeling Jade was well aware of her love for Dominic, although, surprisingly, that was the one thing the two of them had never talked about. Jade was her best friend, but somehow her love for Dominic had always seemed too sensitive a subject to put into words, even to someone as close to her as Jade was. Maybe because she knew that love was so hopeless. The last thing she wanted was pity.

She chanced another glance at Dominic beneath lowered lashes. He looked grim again. What was he thinking about as he drove along so competently? She never had been able to even guess at his thoughts, the façade he showed to the world always enigmatic.

He was probably thinking of something quite mundane—such as how insane the two of them must be to be undertaking this journey at all! It might have been nice, just for once, to imagine they were a little in tune with each other. But, as she knew all too well, Dominic was a past master at hiding his thoughts, and feelings, from everyone.

Although he had certainly shown some reaction to her handing in her resignation, Cathy acknowledged ruefully. Though she certainly wasn't going to attempt to build any more hopeless dreams on *that*.

She closed her eyes determinedly, wishing the journey—and this torture—over. Beyond this lay the warmth of Penny and Simon and their home, the wonder of Jade and David's love for each other, the innocence of her two young nephews as they excitedly looked forward to Christmas.

She smiled at the thoughts, wishing herself there, longing for that enveloping warmth, not aware of the moment when the thoughts became a hazy dream and carried her off to sleep...

'Lunch, Cathy.'

Lunch? What did lunch have to do with the golden vision before her, all the family seated about the brightly lit Christmas tree? But even as the irritated question came to her Dominic appeared in the vision carrying a silver tray of food. And he looked so right there among her family and friends, so incredibly perfect, so——

'I said it's time for lunch, Cathy,' that intrusive voice persisted.

So he kept saying. But she wasn't in the least hungry, and——

'Cathy, wake up.' A firm hand shook her shoulder.

She frowned at the irritation, trying unsuccessfully to shake off the hand, only to have the action repeated, more vigorously this time. 'Go away,' she muttered impatiently.

'You always were bad-tempered when you woke up.' Dominic was amused now.

Cathy was frowning as she reluctantly opened her eyes, the wonderful dream having disappeared as if it had never been. As it hadn't. Dreams were an impossibility.

Dominic was sitting turned towards her in his seat, not the smiling, loving man in her dreams, but the cynic she was more used to.

'You've been asleep almost two hours, and I need some lunch,' he told her practically.

She moved stiffly, still frowning darkly as she straightened in her seat to look around them. Dominic had stopped at one of the roadside service areas, and outside the car the snow still fell softly, thick on the ground where there were no vehicles to churn it up and melt it into muddy slush. The sky was darker above them, too, as if the weight of the snow yet to come was hanging heavily above them.

'Stop complaining, when it was your suggestion that I sleep,' she snapped moodily, looking in the overhead mirror and doing her best to straighten her appearance before they got out.

Dominic smiled at her bad temper, shaking his head. 'Let's go and get something to eat. Fussing over your appearance isn't going to do you a lot of good when you get outside in the wind.'

The coldness outside did a lot to revive her spirits; she had always loved the snow. Large flecks of it landed on her face and hair, and she was gazing up at the featherlight flakes when her footing suddenly seemed to go from under her and she felt herself falling.

'Steady.' Dominic's hand was instantly under her elbow as he kept her on her feet, easily supporting her weight beside him. 'Perhaps you'd better hold on to me.' He put her hand in the crook of his arm and held it there.

During the whole time she had worked for him, Dominic had rarely had a need to touch her, and having his hand against hers now made the cold completely disappear. Cathy suddenly felt too warm for comfort.

As was usual in these places, the service area was noisy and crowded, especially so as it was Christmas Eve, with everyone more than full of the joys of the season as they anticipated the holiday ahead.

The queue for food in the restaurant looked never-ending, and several people were so bored by the wait that they were indulging in horseplay that could only be described as juvenile, one teenage boy very free with his mistletoe as he moved among the queue looking for all the pretty young ladies.

Cathy winced as she glanced sideways at Dominic, knowing from experience that he

hated anything resembling a fast-food restaurant at the best of times. And with the
volume of people that passed through these
service areas in a day they couldn't be classed
as anything else!

But today Dominic didn't seem in the least
concerned by their surroundings. Just as he
seemed totally unaware of the fact that Cathy's
hand was still tucked warmly inside his arm!

'Wow, my luck's really in today,' murmured
an admiring voice.

During her preoccupation with Dominic
Cathy had completely forgotten the young man
with the mistletoe, but unfortunately he seemed
to have reached their place in the queue.

He was a young man of about eighteen, with
an untidy mop of blond hair and mischievous
blue eyes, wearing the customary jeans and
thick jacket.

And he looked as if he had every intention
of kissing her.

'I don't think so,' Dominic drawled softly.

An irritated blue gaze was turned on the
older man as he stood so commandingly at
Cathy's side. The two gazes clashed challengingly but, whatever it was the younger man read
in Dominic's eyes, he looked disappointed
rather than rebellious when he turned back
wistfully towards Cathy.

Then his expression brightened suddenly. 'Well, there's no reason why the mistletoe shouldn't be put to good use.' And he held the green sprig with its creamy berries over Cathy's and Dominic's heads, his intention obvious as he looked at them expectantly.

Cathy was too embarrassed by the action to even glance at Dominic.

How on earth were they going to get out of this one, and with everyone in the near vicinity turning to look at them curiously now? If Dominic tried to cry off by claiming she worked for him he was only likely to receive ribald comments from the over-enthusiastic crowd in here today.

But the idea of the two of them actually kissing each other was unthinkable too!

'I——'

'It *is* Christmas, Cathy,' Dominic reminded her softly, the firmness of his lips softening into a smile as her mouth fell open in surprise at his remark.

The fact that her mouth had fallen open made the brief brushing together of lips that the kiss should have been virtually impossible, their mouths melding together in a kiss that took Cathy's breath away.

Dominic was actually kissing her, was standing in the middle of a crowded restaurant and *kissing* her! It was unreal. Incredible. Beautiful. Wonderful . . .

And over much too soon.

She swayed dizzily, her mouth still raised invitingly as Dominic straightened, looking as cool and in control as he usually did. And for all the world as if he hadn't just shattered Cathy's own control.

The young man with the mistletoe moved off down the queue in the search of more victims of his pranks, having no idea of the turmoil he had left behind him.

The focus was no longer on the two of them, and yet Cathy couldn't speak. Her lips still felt the touch of Dominic's, firm and oh, so sensual, not cold and unyielding as they had always appeared.

She was breathing hard, her fingernails digging into the sleeve of Dominic's jacket where she still clung to his arm, slowly forcing her grip to relax as Dominic looked down at her enquiringly.

'I——' She moistened dry lips. 'I'm sorry about that.'

'It doesn't matter,' he dismissed shruggingly, turning to organise their food on to a tray. 'It didn't hurt.'

It took a couple of minutes for Cathy to realise he was talking about her nails digging into his arm, and not the kiss!

How could he just carry on as if nothing unusual had happened, when to her it had been the single most breathtaking experience of her life? Because *he* wasn't in love, she acknowledged heavily.

But, whatever she had thought of the intimate side of his life during the past few years, the kiss he had given her had been that of an expert, practised and assured. And she was left wondering *who* he had done the practising with!

'You didn't mind what happened just now, did you?' Dominic had turned and seen her frowning expression. 'I thought it would cause less embarrassment to all concerned if we just humoured the young man.'

Of course he had; he certainly hadn't *wanted* to kiss her.

'I realised as much.' She nodded abruptly. 'The chicken looks nice,' she murmured brightly, the slightly dry-looking poultry, despite the sauce that covered it, not really appealing to her at all. In fact, the thought of any food at all made her feel ill.

'Won't you be having enough turkey over Christmas?' Dominic taunted.

More than enough, if the turkeys she remembered Penny buying in the past were anything to go by. The remark about the chicken had just been for something to say rather than any real interest in the subject.

'The chicken, please,' she requested from the lady who was serving up the meals, stubbornly ignoring Dominic's mockery. 'Thank you.' She smiled warmly at the woman before moving on with her tray, picking up a dessert she didn't want either, and a cup of coffee that resembled black tar from sitting in the pot so long. And all the time she studiously avoided showing any interest in the meal Dominic was choosing for himself, although she did note that he hadn't opted for the chicken.

'I'll pay for all this,' he told her as they reached the checkout.

Cathy looked at him coldly. 'I'll pay; we aren't on company expenses now, you know.'

'You——'

'All on one bill, please,' she told the waiting woman firmly, her purse already out of her bag, her expression unyielding as she waited for the total before handing over the money.

'I was only going to say,' said Dominic softly as they moved away in search of an empty table, 'thank you.' He deftly moved in on a table that had recently been vacated.

Cathy gave him a frowning look as she joined him. 'You don't have to go over the top in an effort to try and keep me on as your PA,' she finally drawled dismissively.

He sat back in his chair, looking at her consideringly, his eyes a deep green between thick, dark lashes. 'Is that what I'm doing?'

'Yes,' she snapped, not fooled for a minute; she knew him too well to be taken in. He was being just too amenable. 'And you might as well save yourself the time and effort.'

'It isn't working, hmm?' He grimaced.

'Not in the least,' she assured him triumphantly. Although a few more kisses like the one they had shared a few minutes ago and she would agree to anything!

Cathy took over the driving when they resumed their journey. The snow was still falling softly, although the motorway was being kept quite clear. Nevertheless, the driving conditions were hazardous, and her shoulders, arms and neck all ached from the tension after only a short time behind the wheel.

Not that she was going to admit that to Dominic. He had driven for hours, and she was going to do the same. Especially as he seemed to be taking advantage of his break by catching up on some sleep of his own.

The conditions became increasingly worse once they had turned off the main roads and were trying to follow the country route to Penny and Simon's school, the gritting-lorries and snow-ploughs unable to deal with these minor roads. Even Cathy's eyes ached from the intense concentration she was having to exert to just keep the vehicle on the road.

And then headlights were blazing directly in front of the car, coming straight towards them, and instinctively Cathy turned the wheel sharply to the left.

There was a bumping and grinding noise at the same time, and a thud from overhead as snow from the drift they had ploughed into fell on top of the car.

Cathy was badly shaken for several minutes, breathless, trembling all over. And then she realised Dominic hadn't made a sound during or since the accident. She turned slowly to look at him, almost afraid of what she might see.

She blanched even more as she saw Dominic was unconscious, a trickle of blood coming from one side of his mouth.

CHAPTER THREE

OH, GOD, oh, God, let him be all right, Cathy prayed as she desperately tried to rouse Dominic.

It had taken only seconds to release her own seatbelt, turn and try to get some response from him.

It was only as she gingerly tried to move him that she realised he also had a lump on his forehead that seemed to be growing larger by the second. And he was still unconscious.

Oh, God, she had killed him, had caused Dominic's death because she had been too damned stubborn to wake him up and admit she was too strained to drive any more.

She pulled him against her as she buried her face against his hair. 'Oh, Dominic, I didn't mean to.' She trembled uncontrollably, tears falling unheeded down her cheeks. 'I didn't mean to. Oh, God, what am I going to do? What am I going to *do*?'

'I don't like salt,' he murmured gruffly against her.

Cathy moved back slightly to look down at him wonderingly. 'You're alive!'

But her elation was short-lived as she realised he was also delirious; he had to be. It must be that bang on the head. Lord knew what damage it had done. And they were stuck out here in the middle of nowhere, with not even another car in sight—the idiot who had caused her to swerve in the first place hadn't even stopped to see if they were all right. He either hadn't realised what had happened or else he hadn't cared to stop and find out; either way, he was no help to them.

She stared frantically into Dominic's eyes. Were the pupils supposed to be dilated or not dilated if you were suffering from shock? She couldn't remember. And——

'What are you doing now?' he demanded irritably, straightening in his seat, putting up a tentative hand to his lip and chin, swearing profusely when the hand came away covered in blood.

'Checking your eyes,' Cathy answered distractedly, still trying to remember whether his eyes should be dilated or not. 'And you shouldn't get excited in your condition,' she tried to soothe his temper as he angrily wiped the blood away with a handkerchief.

'What condition?' he scowled, releasing his seatbelt to flex his shoulders experimentally, obviously satisfied with the result as he began to test his limbs. 'And you've chosen a hell of a time to decide to gaze into my eyes!' He turned to push open the door with force, the snowdrift they had half driven into covering the front of the car.

Cathy scrambled out after him as he stepped out into the snow, watching as he began to check the car over. 'And *you* really should sit down! Who knows what damage you've done to yourself?' she fumed worriedly.

'The damage who's done?' He straightened from examining how the left front bumper was resting down against the wheel, preventing its movement in the immediate future. '*I* wasn't the one who drove us into this snowdrift.'

Had she really been overjoyed a few moments ago when she'd realised he was still alive? Of course she had, but did he have to regain consciousness as the same bloody-minded, arrogant——

'But laying the blame on anyone doesn't alter the fact that we're apparently stuck out here in the middle of nowhere.' Dominic looked about them disapprovingly. 'With a car that's completely undriveable.' He glanced up at the heavily laden sky. 'And still a lot more snow to fall, by the look of it.'

He *seemed* lucid now—in fact he seemed more than lucid!—and yet he had been talking so strangely when he came around...

'I think the most important thing at the moment is to get you to a doctor——'

'Doctor?' he repeated sceptically. 'I don't need to see a doctor for this little bump on the——'

'It isn't only the bump,' Cathy cut in firmly. 'It's the bleeding from the mouth that worries me. Who knows what internal damage you've done? Your speech was completely disorientated when you regained consciousness——'

'My dear Cathy,' he interrupted with forceful impatience, 'the bleeding from the mouth can be explained by the fact that my tongue is hurting like hell from the deep gash it has down the side of it where I bit into it on impact—*that's* the only internal damage I have. As for what I was saying when I regained consciousness—if you remember, you were crying all over me, and it was your tears that were salty.'

Cathy stared at him disbelievingly. He managed to make her concern sound childish and unnecessary. Damn it, it *was* unnecessary; this man didn't need anyone's concern. And in future he wasn't going to get any from her!

'I'm so sorry,' she said with only thinly disguised sarcasm. 'The next time we have an accident I'll just sit by and let you bleed to death!'

'There won't be any more accidents,' he rasped. 'Because in future *I'll* drive.'

'You——' She broke off with a deep steadying breath, knowing the criticism was half deserved. 'There was another car driving towards us on the wrong side of the road,' she defended herself emotionally.

'We both know I should have been driving at this stage in the journey.' His eyes were narrowed grimly as he began to take their luggage out of the boot of the car, anger emanating from him in hot waves.

'You were asleep——'

'I could have been woken.' He slammed the boot shut with a resounding bang, everything about them seeming unnaturally quiet in the darkness of the evening.

Cathy knew she had no answer to the accusations. She was well aware of the fact that she shouldn't have been driving when the accident happened, that she had passed the point of tiredness long ago and quickly gone on to exhaustion. 'Where are we going now?' She frowned as Dominic brought their coats out from the interior of the car before locking the doors.

He shrugged into his jacket. 'Wherever we can find shelter.' He tested the torch he had taken out of the boot with the luggage; as expected, it worked perfectly.

'I noticed a driveway about half a mile back. I think,' she added lamely. She had already made such a mess of things that searching for a non-existent driveway was sure to make Dominic's temper explode completely. But she was more or less certain she *had* seen one a short way back—hadn't she...?

Dominic had already picked up the majority of their luggage, and Cathy couldn't help giving an inward groan as the beam from the torch he held illuminated the huge lump that had appeared on his forehead, a purple bruising already appearing on the swollen skin. It really should be professionally looked at, despite what Dominic said to the contrary, although she didn't dare suggest that at the moment. She didn't want to be accused of crying 'salty' tears all over him again!

She just *hoped* she was right about that driveway!

She was, although the distance was more like a mile, through snow that was knee-high in places, with the flakes still falling icily, and when they finally did find it the house at the end of the driveway didn't look inhabited, having not a single light shining in any of the windows.

And they soon discovered why. 'Southview Holiday Cottage', the sign on the front door read. And obviously no one had rented it for the *Christmas* holiday!

'Well, that's that, then.' Cathy sat down wearily on her case, too exhausted to walk any further for the moment. Besides, she hadn't seen any other driveways but this one for miles. And it was eerily dark now, and the snow just kept falling, with no traffic having passed this way during the time it had taken them to walk the mile. The police had been giving out warnings on the radio for the last hour about road closures; it would be just their luck if this was now one of them!

Dominic turned to her in the darkness. 'Did you see any other houses nearby?'

'No,' she answered without hesitation. 'I don't think so,' she amended doubtfully. 'I don't know,' she finished awkwardly.

She was tired, exhausted actually, and if she was right about this being one of the roads that was now classed as impassable then she didn't know when they were ever going to get out of this cold and snow. She gave an involuntary shudder.

'Then we have no choice,' Dominic said grimly, and the luggage he carried thudded into the snow at his feet.

'What are you doing?' Cathy frowned as he turned away and she heard the tinkling of glass.

'Breaking in,' he answered without the least trace of remorse.

Her exhaustion became a thing of the past as she shot to her feet, her eyes wide in disbelief. 'You can't do that!'

'I already have,' he mocked, the door swinging inwards seconds later. A flick of a switch and the light from the hallway shone golden out on to the snow. Dominic stood in the doorway looking back at her with the snow almost reaching her knees. 'Well, aren't you coming in?' he finally drawled when she made no move to go in out of the driving snow. 'Or do your obviously shocked sensibilities mean you intend staying out there all night?' He turned away uninterestedly, going off to investigate the cottage on his own.

'Dominic!' she halted him, stumbling inelegantly through the snow. He was watching her with raised brows over amused green eyes by the time she finally reached the doorway. 'We can't simply—*walk* into someone else's property like this,' she protested lamely.

'We didn't walk in, I broke in,' he corrected calmly before resuming his progress down the hallway, leaving wet footprints on the carpet behind him.

'Where are you going now?' Cathy gasped.

'To see what, if any, provisions are in the kitchen,' he told her without pausing.

They couldn't do this, not just break in— Dominic's description *was* the correct one!—

and make themselves at home in someone else's house! Without the slightest qualm at doing so on Dominic's part, it seemed. He hadn't even hesitated, beyond that brief question about other habitation. He could be the most arrogant of men, but she had never——

'The way I look at it, Cathy, we have two choices.' The rasp of Dominic's voice harshly interrupted her troubled thoughts, and as she looked up and saw him standing darkly at the end of the hallway she realised that her shock over his actions had affected him after all. 'We can either sit outside in the snow and freeze to death while the shelter we need so badly is just a locked door away——' his voice remained hard and unyielding even though he must have seen the way her face blanched '—or we can break in—— ' his head was thrown back challengingly, his hair appearing raven-black in the dull overhead lighting '—and hope that there is an electric fire or alternatively that we can find something to burn so that we don't die of hypothermia anyway!'

Typical Dominic; neither option held much appeal.

Although he was right about the cold inside the cottage: it wasn't much of an improvement on the outside. But then it was just a holiday cottage, and probably hadn't been rented out for months.

'For God's sake, woman,' Dominic bit out impatiently. 'If we survive this I'll make sure the owner is suitably recompensed for the damage I've done, and for the use of the place.'

Of course he would; he could easily buy the cottage if it came to that.

But the way he kept mentioning that there was a possibility they wouldn't make it out of this storm made her feel awash with guilt; after all, if it hadn't been for her they wouldn't be here at all. And Dominic wouldn't have that discoloured lump on his forehead, that faint trace of dried blood at the corner of his mouth, and they wouldn't be in danger of freezing to death before morning.

Knowing how brutally honest Dominic could be, Cathy was surprised he hadn't pointed that out to her before now!

'I'm not about to argue with you,' he dismissed tersely as she still didn't make any reply. 'I intend to spend the night in this cottage, such as it is. You'll just have to do your own wrestling between your common sense and your conscience.'

Put in such blunt terms—the way only Dominic could!—what choice did she have?

One of the first things they were going to have to do, Cathy realised as she closed the door behind her, was block up the hole Dominic had made in one of the small panes of glass at the top of the door so that they could get in; the wind and snow whirling through it at the moment certainly weren't going to do anything to alleviate the cold that already existed inside!

It was quite a pleasantly decorated and furnished cottage, Cathy noticed abstractedly as she glanced in doorways on her way down the hall to the kitchen. Only the bare essentials, like most of these types of places, but adequate, none the less. And, she noticed with some relief, there was an electric fire standing in front of the open fireplace in the lounge. Now all she had to hope for was that it worked.

It did!

Their situation instantly began to seem improved as the artificial coals glowed cheerfully and the two elements began to glow red.

Dominic was still poking about in cupboards when she bounded gleefully into the kitchen to clasp his arm and pull his resisting form towards the sitting-room. 'Come and see,' she said persuasively.

'This is serious, Cathy——'

'I know that,' she said exasperatedly. 'But look!' She proudly showed off the glowing electric fire that had already taken the chill off the room in the few minutes she had been gone. 'What are you doing?' she demanded disbelievingly as he strode across the room to switch the fire off.

He looked grim as he straightened. 'I noticed the fire when I first entered the cottage.'

'Then——'

'I also saw,' he continued forcefully, 'the electricity meter in the hallway where you have to put fifty-pence pieces to get the electricity supply,' he explained derisively. 'I don't have enough fifty-pence pieces to keep that,' he nodded in the direction of the cooling fire, 'running for very long—do you?'

Heated colour flooded her cheeks at his withering tone. She might have the odd one or two fifty-pence pieces in her handbag, but she doubted she had any more than that. How was she supposed to have known it wasn't the normal electricity supply? The same way Dominic had, a mocking little voice in her head tormented: by observation.

Dominic's mouth twisted as he looked through the change from his pocket, finding two of the necessary coins. 'Obviously the owner only put enough money into the meter to keep the thing ticking over until the next rental, because when I checked there were only a couple of units left on it.'

'The lights...?' she suddenly realised with dismay, expecting at any moment to be plunged into darkness again.

'The lights are fine,' Dominic dismissed. 'They hardly use any electricity at all; it's just the fire we'll have to use sparingly.' He put the coins in the meter and turned the handle. 'Come into the kitchen and I'll show you what I've found in there so far.'

It couldn't be very much; it was a very small kitchen!

In that, at least, she was correct. For all that she was, in all modesty, an excellent personal assistant, she would have made a lousy Girl Friday!

Only a small supply of tea and coffee had been left in the cottage, obviously in readiness for the next holiday season; there was no food at all.

'And I found these in the cleaning cupboard under the sink.' Dominic held up a box of candles.

Cathy stared at them blankly for several seconds, frowning as she accepted that, instead of their intended use in an emergency if there was an electricity failure, these candles could become their only source of lighting as soon as the electricity meter ran out. For the first time she wished she had followed Penny's example and joined the Girl Guides; at least then she might have had some idea of how to survive in a situation like this, would perhaps know how to light a fire without matches——

'Oh, God, matches!' She groaned her dismay as realisation dawned that neither of them smoked and so were unlikely to be carrying matches around with them.

'They were next to the candles, fortunately.' To her relief Dominic pulled a box of matches out of the cleaning cupboard too. 'In fact,' he added drily, 'this cupboard is the most well-stocked in the room: polish, washing-up liquid, some sort of fluid to clean the floor——'

'I don't suppose they wanted to give anyone the excuse not to clean up after their stay here,' Cathy derided.

'If that's another dig at me——'

'It wasn't,' she assured him wryly. 'But I'm sure that all the owners would be interested in was receiving their money and making sure the cottage was kept in a clean condition for the next lot of people to stay here.'

Dominic's expression was grim. 'Then let's hope we aren't stuck here for too long; we don't appear to have any food,' he explained at her questioning look. 'And while the steak I had at lunchtime was adequate, that was several hours ago.'

'Dominic——'

'By breakfast tomorrow you'll be impossible to live with,' he realised with a frown.

'Dominic——' She patiently tried to talk again, ignoring his reference to her eating habits.

'You know you will, Cathy.' He sighed heavily. 'If you aren't fed at regular intervals your temper suffers—and so does everyone around you.'

'Dominic!' She spoke more firmly this time.

'It's ridiculous how we know more about each other in ways like that than a lot of married couples seem to do.' He scowled.

Because for the past five years they had lived closer together than a lot of married couples were ever able to, Cathy acknowledged achingly. But a married couple was something they weren't and never would be...

'I have been trying to tell you for the last few minutes,' she spoke sharply in her agitation, 'that the immediate problem about food is easily solvable.'

He nodded abruptly. 'I realise we'll have no trouble surviving for a couple of days——'

'That is, of course,' Cathy continued as if he had never spoken, 'if you don't mind living on cold roast ham and other assorted meats, plus some fine cheeses and wines, and——'

'Cathy, what are you babbling about?' he interrupted impatiently. 'It's much too soon for you to be delirious!' he added dismissively.

'I'm not delirious.' She chuckled softly. 'Just grateful that Simon has a weakness for cooked meats and fine cheeses——'

'Cathy——'

'Dominic,' she returned mockingly. 'Tell me, just what did you think I had in that wicker case you so kindly carried here for me?'

'How the hell would I know?' he scowled. 'Although, from the weight of it, I presumed it had to be clothes!'

'For your information, we have our supper and breakfast in there at least,' she announced triumphantly, relieved to feel that she was at last contributing something constructive to what could so far only be called a disaster.

She lifted the wicker case up on to a worktop, slipping the clasps to lift the lid. Inside the hamper it was like an Aladdin's cave of food and wines.

She turned back to Dominic excitedly. 'I stopped and bought this for Penny and Simon on my way in to the office this morning. I wasn't supposed to be in today at all,' she told him defensively at his raised brows. Honestly, she had just presented him with food for their unexpected stopover here, and all he could think about was the fact that she had been late getting in because of it!

'No, only to hand in your notice, it seems,' he rasped. 'So,' he bit out tersely, 'at least we stand a chance of not starving to death before help arrives. Now we just have the problem of hypothermia.'

The elated realisation that she had been able to supply them with the much-needed food faded as she looked about the stark desolation of the cottage.

It was a far cry from the Christmas she had imagined for herself this year.

She knew she would have been missing Dominic very badly by now if she had made it to Penny and Simon's, but she would have the consolation of family and loving friends, something she had been away from for too long. Now she had Dominic alone for Christmas instead, but a Dominic just as cold and hard as he was the rest of the year.

'What is it?' Dominic had been watching the changing expressions flitting across her face.

She shrugged, trying to smile and failing miserably. 'It isn't exactly the Christmas I had planned for myself,' she admitted wearily.

His mouth tightened, his eyes like hard green pebbles. 'It isn't exactly the Christmas any of us had planned for ourselves. But we'll just have to put up with each other, won't we?'

'I didn't mean——'

'It doesn't really matter what you meant, Cathy,' he rasped. 'The truth of the matter is we're stuck here and we'll both just have to damn well make the best of it!' He strode forcefully out of the kitchen.

Cathy felt as if he had physically slapped her. God knew the situation was bad enough without the two of them insulting each other. And it hadn't been her idea that he drive her down to Devon, damn it, that had been his own arrogance. No one could have foreseen the accident that had rendered the car undriveable. Could she help it that Dominic was now stuck with her for goodness knew how long—and was obviously hating every minute of it?

CHAPTER FOUR

AFTER the explosive end to their conversation, Cathy didn't feel like facing Dominic again straight away. She heard him moving about in the lounge as she went up the stairs to explore the accommodation there.

It comprised three small bedrooms, once again furnished with only the bare essentials; it certainly couldn't be advertised as 'luxurious accommodation'! And there was no bedlinen but a few duvets. It was to be expected, of course; most people preferred to sleep in their own sheets where possible.

But the consistent lack of any real creature-comforts, such as warm bedlinen, made her wonder exactly where she and Dominic were going to sleep.

'In here, of course,' Dominic told her when she questioned him about it.

He was still in the lounge, having moved the electric fire to one side to reveal an open fire-place behind it.

Of course, she mocked self-derisively, where else would they sleep?

'It's the only room that will have any warmth at all,' Dominic continued distractedly. 'That is, it will have if I can find anything we can burn.' He frowned.

'I glanced outside while I was upstairs looking at the bedrooms.' Cathy repressed a shudder at the memory of the unblemished blanket of snow she had seen in the moonlight outside; it had just increased her feelings of desolation. 'I could see a shed of some sort at the back of the cottage,' she supplied what she hoped would be helpful information.

He nodded. 'I'll go out and check inside it. If the worst comes to the worst, I suppose we could always burn the shed itself.'

Cathy wished he were joking, but she knew by the grim determination of his expression that he wasn't. And what if it did come to that? Dominic could replace the shed too, after all.

He was very adept at setting his world to rights with money. At least he hadn't completely insulted her earlier today and offered her money if she would continue to work for him—although the offer of those shares had to be classed as a definite bribe.

Strange, she frowned, she had never noticed before just *how* much Dominic used the power of his money to get what he wanted.

'Don't worry,' he drawled at her expression. 'I'll only resort to that as a drastic measure. In the meantime, why don't you see about getting out the "cold roast ham and other assorted meats, plus some fine cheeses and wines" so that we can have a supper of some kind when I get back?'

You man, me woman, Cathy thought ruefully as she began to unpack the assortment of foods.

Besides the roast ham there was also smoked salmon, pâté, roast beef, the cheeses, assorted pickles, ginger in syrup, tins of fruit, a box of delicious-looking marzipans and mints, half a dozen bottles of wine and, of all things, a jar of popcorn.

The hamper had been designed to enhance Christmas, not make up the sole fare, and it seemed a strange mixture to put out on plates for them to choose from. But at least the wines were good and might help them to digest the food. At least they wouldn't have to worry about using up some of their precious electricity on keeping the food refrigerated; the cottage itself was like an icebox!

Dominic hadn't returned to the cottage by the time she had put the selection of food out, and so she went out into the hallway to try and block up the hole in the glass part of the door with a piece of cardboard from the back of the marzipan box. It wasn't too successful, but at least the wind volume had been reduced slightly.

But Dominic still wasn't back—had been gone almost half an hour now. Surely it didn't take that long to break into the shed—he certainly seemed to be getting a lot of practice at that tonight—and looking around for something they could burn on the fire?

Of course it didn't, she realised worriedly!

Oh, God, perhaps that bump he had received on the head had been serious, after all? She shouldn't have left it this long before checking up on him.

She rushed out into the darkness, the light from the kitchen window and open doorway guiding her down the garden, although it seemed eerily silent as she approached the dark bulk of the shed.

What on earth was she going to do if Dominic had collapsed out here somewhere? He was much too big and heavy for her to drag back down to the cottage.

God, he could have been lying out here in the snow unconscious the whole time she had been pottering around inside the cottage, getting colder and colder, closer and closer to——

'Oh!' She let out a distressed cry as she collided with a solid mass that had appeared in front of her, giving a shaky sigh of relief as she realised it was Dominic's chest she had walked into.

'What the——?'

'Oh, God, it's you! It's you!' she gasped, clasping hold of his arms.

'Of course it's me,' he answered impatiently. 'Who were you expecting, the Abominable Snowman?'

His sarcasm angered her after the concern she had had for his welfare. 'What on earth have you been doing out here?' she demanded heatedly.

His eyes narrowed in the torchlight he had flicked on between them. 'Perhaps it's slipped your memory,' he rasped, 'but I came out here to look for coal or wood.'

'That was ages ago,' she accused, her relief at finding he was all right after all turning into anger in the face of his complete disregard for her feelings. But then, when had it ever been any different?

He nodded abruptly. 'It took a little longer than I anticipated——'

'Did you find any?' she cut in waspishly, still trembling slightly from the fear she had felt for his safety only minutes earlier.

'Some coal,' he answered dismissively. 'Enough to last a few days, anyway.'

'Then maybe you could bring some of it inside and we can get a fire going?' She turned away angrily.

Dominic's hand on her arm halted her, before he swung her round to face him. 'I realise you're getting hungry,' he bit out forcefully. 'But that's no reason for you to——'

'My hunger has nothing to do with my mood,' she blazed, grey eyes shooting flames. 'I was angry for quite another reason. But I wouldn't want to bore you again with my concern for you!' She glared up at him challengingly.

His face, all hard planes and angles in the torchlight, softened to a gentleness that was rarely seen. 'This hasn't been much fun for you so far, has it?' he acknowledged ruefully.

Cathy shrugged, a little of the tension leaving her body. 'It wasn't meant to be fun. After all, I'm the one who drove into the snowdrift and damaged the car so that we couldn't go on any further.'

'The conditions would probably have stopped us doing that anyway very shortly. And don't forget the car driving on the wrong side of the road,' he said softly. 'You couldn't have foreseen that.'

'It was a mythical car, according to you,' she reminded him tautly.

'I never said that.' He shook his head. 'Only that I should have been driving at the time.'

'And, naturally, you would have taken a different evasive action,' she sighed.

'No.' He turned away to pick up the bucket of coal he had ready.

'No?' Cathy repeated incredulously, frowning up at him as they walked back to the cottage.

'No,' he repeated in an amused voice, standing to one side as he waited for her to enter the cottage ahead of him.

'But——'

'Hm, the food looks good,' he murmured in passing. 'And I wouldn't have taken *any* evasive action unless it looked absolutely necessary at the last minute; the other driver should have been the one who got stuck in the snowdrift.' He began to lay the fire.

Her response to the headlights blazing directly in her path had been one of gut reaction, swinging the wheel instinctively to the left. But maybe Dominic was right and if she had waited just a few seconds more they wouldn't have been the ones off the road and in this predicament.

Dominic had a small blaze going in the fireplace, the sticks he had found catching light fast, the hot flames licking about the coal.

He looked up at her. 'How about putting me a selection of food on a plate while I nurse this along a while longer?'

So much for the decorative display she had arranged in the kitchen! But what difference did it really make, as long as they ate?

'Your brother-in-law doesn't know what he's missing,' Dominic told her appreciatively after several mouthfuls of the food and an enjoyable sip of the wine.

'Yes, he does,' Cathy grimaced. 'I told him over the phone that I was bringing the hamper down.'

Dominic returned the smile, then sobered suddenly. 'Your family are going to be worried.'

She had already thought of that, but there was no telephone at the cottage, and no other means of communication either—otherwise they wouldn't still be here! But she had decided there was little point in her worrying about it too; at least *she* knew she was all right.

'I'll walk back down to the car soon and leave a message inside saying where we are——'

'No!' she cried out in panic; she couldn't bear it if something happened to him. Not working for him was one thing, having him ill or possibly worse was something else completely.

He gave a puzzled frown. 'It shouldn't take me that long—— '

'I said no, Dominic,' she cut in with fierce determination.

'If you're worried about being left here on your own——'

'You have to be the most insensitive man alive!' Cathy stood up with her plate still in her hands and walked out of the room, her breath coming in shaky gasps as she leant back against one of the kitchen cabinets, her head bowed.

'Cathy...?'

She turned sharply, her head going back challengingly as she met Dominic's eyes. 'Have you come in here to insult me again?' She attacked instinctively.

He gave a rueful grimace. 'I didn't realise I had the first time.'

'That's the trouble with you,' she bit out waspishly.

'I thought the trouble with me was that I'm the most insensitive man alive,' he drawled derisively.

Hot colour darkened her cheeks, but she refused to be bowed by it. 'You are,' she insisted firmly. 'You're also——'

'Enough,' he cried off with a grin. 'I have to make that trip now really if I'm going.' He glanced out of the window. 'It looks like more snow. I should think the bookmakers have taken a pounding on the chances of a white Christmas this year.' He began to pull on his thick jacket.

'That's right,' Cathy followed him agitatedly to the door, 'make light of the whole thing!'

Dominic turned with a sigh. 'Think sensibly, Cathy,' he reasoned. 'Help could be passing us by on the road not half a mile away, but they just don't know where we are.'

As far as she was concerned they could be stranded here until the thaw if it meant Dominic wasn't to endanger himself! 'I've been *sensible* for five years,' she told him heatedly, 'arranged your schedule, helped juggle your business empire with one hand while answering your telephone with the other, lived and breathed your damned business. Isn't it time you did something for me?' Her eyes blazed with emotion.

'I thought I was,' he returned quietly.

It was because *her* family would be worried that he was doing this; he had no family to worry about him, she realised with a guilty pang. But even so...

Her brow creased in a thoughtful frown. 'Let's compromise,' she finally said with a frown. 'Don't go back to the car tonight; go tomorrow, if you feel you must.'

'And if the weather is worse by then?'

Cathy shrugged. 'Then you don't go.'

He gave a rueful smile. 'That doesn't sound like much of a compromise to me.'

'That's because you——'

'Not another criticism, Cathy!' He sounded exasperated. 'I didn't realise I was so impossible.'

Impossible. Infuriating. More often than not unappreciative. But she loved him anyway.

'Oh, but you are,' she assured him lightly. 'And you don't know the meaning of the word "compromise".'

He grimaced. 'Perhaps not, but I have a feeling you might be going to try and teach it to me.'

To her chagrin her cheeks felt hot with colour at the near-intimacy of his words. But she had to have been imagining that; she was just making a fool of herself by blushing like a schoolgirl.

'Whatever are you going to do without a telephone, Dominic?' she taunted as she stacked their empty plates. 'You'll suffer from withdrawal symptoms!'

He gave an irritated frown. 'You make me sound like a workaholic.'

She smiled. 'I would have thought that was the greatest compliment anyone could have paid you.'

Green eyes narrowed. 'You don't have much of an opinion of me, do you?'

Cathy looked at him in some surprise. 'I consider you to be one of the most brilliant men I've ever met,' she answered slowly.

His mouth twisted. 'Businessmen,' he clarified drily.

Her brows rose. 'What else is there?'

'What indeed?' He gave an abrupt inclination of his head. 'OK, Cathy, I'll go down to the car tomorrow if it makes you happier,' he bit out tersely. 'But I do it on the understanding that, if the weather conditions are too bad by then for me to venture out, it was your idea I should wait.' He threw off his coat again.

A step down for him, with a sting in its tail: she had to realise she was responsible for the decision. It was typical of Dominic. But she didn't care who had to take the responsibility, as long as Dominic didn't go out into the bleakness of the night with the snow still falling. The horrific picture that briefly formed in her mind of him perhaps stranded and helpless out there in that blinding snow was enough to confirm the need for her stubbornness. She didn't give a damn if Dominic was only agreeing under protest.

'*If* I did manage to get help, there's a possibility that you could be with your family tomorrow after all,' he pointed out softly.

If he managed to get help... Even the minutest chance of failure was enough to make her shudder!

'The risk is too great tonight. I would rather we both got out of this alive, thank you,' she told him irritably.

He shrugged broad shoulders. 'Just don't say I didn't offer. I don't want this to be something else for you to throw up in my face in the future.'

She drew herself up angrily. 'Since I doubt very much that we will see each other in the "future", the possibility of that seems very remote!'

His eyes narrowed to green slits, and Cathy could feel the cold fury emanating from him as they faced each other across the width of the room. But she didn't care about his anger; all she cared about was keeping him safe, for tonight at least.

'Besides,' she added tauntingly, 'why should I have your death on my conscience?'

And how's that to be going on with? she mused furiously as she banged about in the kitchen tidying away the debris from the meal. Not that she meant it for a minute, but the nerve of the man!

'I think I'll just go back outside and get some more coal in for the night.'

Cathy had been so intent on her angry thoughts, making so much noise as she threw the dirty plates into the water in the sink, that she hadn't been aware of Dominic's presence close behind her. She was so startled that the plate she had been holding dropped out of her hand back into the water, splashing a large dollop of the soapy bubbles into the air before it landed partly on her face and partly down the front of her jumper.

She looked down at herself in utter stupefaction, made aware of the ridiculousness of the whole situation even as she became aware of how silly she must look with soap bubbles dripping off her; what on earth were they arguing for, when who knew what tomorrow might bring? If there was a tomorrow for them at all...

'I shouldn't be long,' Dominic murmured quietly, leaving the kitchen before she could make any response.

Cathy gazed sightlessly out of the blackness of the window in front of her as she mechanically washed the plates and placed them in the drying tray, the tears falling unchecked down her cheeks. She had never felt so miserable.

She had made a conscious decision to separate her life from Dominic's, the hardest decision she had ever had to make in her life, a decision that was slowly but surely breaking her heart, and yet here they were in the middle of nowhere verbally ripping each other to shreds. How *could* she have made that remark about his death being on her conscience? If anything happened to him she would want to die too; that was the reason she was so determined he shouldn't go out in the cold and darkness tonight.

It was this vulnerability that was slowly destroying her.

She deliberately kept her back towards him as she heard him re-enter the kitchen, knowing beyond a shadow of a doubt that her vulnerability was written all over her face.

'I know it isn't much,' he murmured softly. 'But I thought it might help.'

Cathy turned with a frown, the frown deepening as she saw the small conifer in a bucket of earth that he held in his arms.

'I saw it peeping up through the top of the snow in the garden, and digging it up to bring into the cottage seemed like a good idea at the time,' he added with a grimace as she continued to stare at him. 'That was what was taking me so long earlier.' He shrugged. 'I realise it's a bit small to be a Christmas tree, but I thought it might look passable with a little decoration on it.'

Cathy looked from Dominic's hard, masculine frame to the two-foot-high conifer he held in his arms, and then back again.

It hardly seemed possible that he had gone to all that trouble for *her*. And only a few minutes ago she had been talking so scathingly about his death!

With a choked sob she turned and fled from the room.

CHAPTER FIVE

THE bedroom was icy cold, the mattress damp, but Cathy didn't notice any of that as she sat down heavily on top of the bed, the almost uncontrollable sobs shaking her body.

'I didn't mean to make you cry.'

She turned sharply as Dominic sat down on the bed next to her. 'You didn't,' she sniffled, rubbing agitatedly at the tears on her cheeks, tensing stiffly as Dominic's arm came about her shoulders.

'It's been quite a day one way or another, hasn't it?' he mused ruefully.

She gave a choked laugh at the understatement. 'You could say that!'

'I just did,' he derided drily, his fingers gentle beneath her chin as he turned her to look at him. 'I don't think I've ever seen you cry before.' He frowned searchingly.

'Today *has* been a different kind of day,' she reminded him.

Dominic nodded abruptly. 'It certainly has,' he acknowledged gruffly. 'But how about we try and salvage something from it and go and see what we can find to put on that minute tree——?'

'It's a beautiful tree,' she defended it fiercely. 'The most beautiful tree I've ever seen!'

He gave a teasing smile. 'I think that may be a bit of an exaggeration!'

Cathy looked up at him, loving him all the more at that moment. She had always believed he was human under that hard façade; she could only wish helplessly that she hadn't been proved so right at a time when she was so vulnerable. It would be so easy to reach up and put her arms about his neck and pull his head down to hers. In fact, it was what her arms ached to do.

And Dominic would probably be shocked out of his mind if she did that!

She stood up abruptly. 'It's cold up here,' she dismissed abruptly.

Dominic watched her wordlessly for several long seconds before he stood up. 'I suppose we should go and see what, if anything, we can do with that tree,' he conceded ruefully.

To Cathy it really was the most beautiful tree she had ever seen, she acknowledged as they used the red ribbon that had adorned the hamper, and popped some of the corn to put on the tiny green branches. It certainly wasn't the biggest or the grandest tree she had ever seen, but it was, quite simply, a gift from Dominic she had never expected.

Her cheeks were flushed with pleasure as the tree took pride of place on the coffee-table in the lounge. The ribbon and the popcorn did little to hide the fact that it was a baby conifer hardly strong enough to sustain even that slight weight, and yet it was a symbol of a gentleness within Dominic that up until now Cathy had only dared to hope for.

Dominic looked at it consideringly, unaware of her emotion. 'A few coloured lights might have made it halfway presentable——'

'It's perfect as it is,' Cathy insisted firmly.

Green eyes glinted with laughter. 'And let no one say any different, hm?'

Her head went back with mock challenge as she fell in with his light-hearted mood. 'Not unless he's a very brave man.'

His lips twitched. 'I'm not *that* brave!'

'I should hope not,' she said with feigned haughtiness.

'Wine?' Dominic prompted gently.

In truth, she was still feeling a little heady from the wine they had drunk earlier with their meal, but the moment was too perfect for her not to want it to continue, too poignantly rare and beautiful not to be a memory she would cherish for a very long time to come.

'Mm, please,' she accepted with a nod, her voice husky.

'I won't be long,' he told her softly. 'At least we don't have any problem keeping the wine chilled,' he added ruefully.

Cathy sat and stared at the flickering of the fire as she waited for him to come back with the wine. The flames danced and played, flirting tantalisingly, just as her dreams of herself and Dominic together had merely flirted with reality.

Those dreams... How wonderful they had seemed at the time. She couldn't have guessed how far out of her reach they would always be.

'I really will get us away from here as soon as possible,' Dominic told her frowningly as he placed two glasses and the bottle of wine down on the table before joining her on the sofa.

Cathy broke her gaze away from the mesmerising fascination of the flames to look up at Dominic dazedly for several seconds as she tried to absorb what he had just said to her.

She shook her head. 'It really doesn't matter,' she dismissed. 'I'd stopped even thinking about it,' she added as she realised he must have thought that was why she was so quiet.

'Then why did you look so sad?'

'Did I?' she said brightly—too brightly! 'Maybe I'm just tired.'

That hadn't been the right thing to say either! Tiredness meant bed, and they were both going to have to sleep in this room tonight. She was no coy young girl to cower and balk at the thought, especially when it was such a necessity, but events had been such today that she was so vulnerable...

Dominic ran his hand tiredly around the back of his nape. 'It certainly has been one hell of a day,' he grimaced with feeling.

Cathy smiled at him teasingly, determined to regain some of the spirit that had kept her— and her self-respect—intact the last five futile years. 'Poor Dominic,' she mocked. 'Having the PA you personally trained leave you, and then, to make matters worse, being forced to acknowledge that most dreaded of seasons in such a basically commercial way as a Christmas tree!'

He turned his head slightly so that he could look at the tree as it stood so nobly proud in its makeshift adornment. 'There's nothing in the least commerical about that tree,' he said huskily. 'In fact, this is the closest I've come to enjoying a Christmas for more years than I——' He broke off abruptly, shaking his head, his mouth twisting ruefully. 'Here I am actually enjoying it, and in terms of what you wanted it's a disaster for you!'

Cathy looked at him frowningly. Could he really be enjoying this impromptu Christmas?

She had learnt from hard-won experience that Dominic rarely said anything he didn't mean, so it had to be true, amazing as it might seem. And amazing it certainly was!

'Wine, I think,' he announced determinedly before she could make any verbal response, sitting forward to pour two glassfuls of the golden liquid. 'Happy Christmas, Cathy,' he teased, his gaze warm in the firelight. 'And I really mean that.'

She could see that, could feel herself being drawn towards him. She took a hasty sip of her wine and choked as it caught unexpectedly in her throat.

Dominic patted her firmly on the back as she spluttered and coughed. 'Now you know how all those other people must have felt when Scrooge did an about-face,' he mocked as her breathing slowly calmed.

Guilty colour flooded her cheeks. 'I was very angry when I made that remark,' she defended.

'As hell,' he acknowledged drily, relaxing back on the sofa.

Cathy sipped her wine more carefully the second time. 'What is your middle name?'

He shook his head. 'Classified information.'

She gave him an indignant look. 'I've worked for you for five years and I still don't know it!'

He quirked taunting eyebrows. 'Reconsider your notice and I might think about telling you.'

'I'm not *that* interested,' she told him haughtily.

'No?' he taunted, very relaxed as he slouched down on the sofa, absently twirling his wine glass between long, tapered fingers.

She had to admit—to herself, at least—that his reluctance to reveal his middle name had been something that had intrigued her for a long time. But not to the extent of actually returning to work for him to find out what it was! 'No,' she dismissed offhandedly.

'More wine?' He refilled her glass. 'It will help keep you warm,' he excused at her raised brows.

It was also making her more sleepy than ever, her eyelids drooping tiredly. 'Shouldn't we start thinking about making up some beds and trying to get some sleep?' she suggested abruptly.

'Bed,' he corrected lightly.

The tiredness vanished as if a bucket of icy snow had been thrown over her. 'I don't——'

'This sofa makes up into a bed, Cathy,' he informed her in a brisk voice that brooked no arguments. 'I have no intention of sleeping in a chair when there's a perfectly good bed available.'

She put her glass down with a loud thud. 'You're such a gentleman!' Her eyes blazed.

'Being a gentleman doesn't come into it.'

'I couldn't agree more!'

'Damn it, Cathy,' he rasped, his eyes narrowed impatiently, 'you aren't a schoolgirl, to be shocked at the thought of sharing your bed with a man.'

She wasn't a schoolgirl, no, but the thought of sharing a bed with a man, any man, not just Dominic, did panic her a little.

Her early teenage years had been spent going on the usual harmless dates with boys of her own age, and her latter teens had been spent mainly studying, with barely time to think about men, let alone to have fully fledged affairs with any of them. And then she had met Dominic and the time for any affairs, love or otherwise, had passed her by in her feelings for him.

At the age of twenty-six she had *never* shared a bed with any man, even platonically. And she wasn't sure *that* was possible, on her part, with Dominic being the man she loved above everything and everyone else.

'I didn't say I was,' she returned defensively, standing up with uncoordinated agitation. 'But if you won't sleep in the chair, I will!'

Dominic stood up too, tension in every line of his body. 'You've become damned unreasonable recently, a little she-cat who spits and claws for no good reason.'

'In *your* opinion,' she snapped. '*I* think I have every reason.'

'Exactly—you're unreasonable!'

They stood glaring at each other for at least a minute, until Cathy, at least, began to see the funny side of the situation. What on earth were they doing, shouting at each other and carrying on in this way? They were *both* unreasonable.

Dominic relaxed slightly as she gave a rueful smile, and shook his head. 'This might be hackneyed, and as clichéd as hell, but you're beautiful when you're angry.'

The words might never have been spoken before as far as Cathy was concerned; all that mattered to her was that Dominic had said she was beautiful.

Her gaze was locked with his. 'Maybe I should have got angry more often.' Her voice was husky.

He nodded, his own gaze unwavering. 'Maybe you should.'

'I——' She swallowed hard at the sudden tension that crackled between them. 'Dominic, what's happening?' she asked uncertainly, voicing her thoughts.

'Does it really matter?' He was standing in front of her now.

It mattered more than anything else ever had in her life before. But the situation was fast whirling out of control, and that kiss Dominic had given her at the service restaurant earlier in the day paled into insignificance at the burning passion that ignited between them as soon as their lips met.

Cathy trembled with the intensity of the emotion, holding on to Dominic's shoulders to steady herself as she swayed. And then she wasn't holding on to him at all but twining her arms up about his neck, her fingers entwined in his hair, silky soft hair that was infinitely sensual to the touch. As was the feel of his body pressed against her, hard, remorseless flesh that fitted against hers so perfectly.

His tongue danced a pattern against her lips before seeking entry, and Cathy's body gave a trembling response.

She had to stop this while she still had enough sanity left to do it!

She wrenched her mouth away from his, breathing hard, her eyes dark grey pools of confusion. 'What are you doing?' she gasped breathlessly.

His lips travelled down the column of her throat. 'I know it's been a long time for me,' he murmured gruffly, 'but I didn't think I was that out of practice.'

She didn't care how long ago it was since he had held a woman like this; the fact was, it was *she* whom he was holding now—and her defences were crumbling fast.

'You don't work for me any more, Cathy,' he encouraged softly.

She frowned, although it was difficult to think coherently when he was nibbling at the side of her mouth with his lips. 'What difference does that make?' she managed to ask raggedly.

'None at all to me,' he dismissed drily. 'I just thought it might make you feel more comfortable. Do you think we could stop talking now? I can think of much nicer things we could be doing.'

Cathy wouldn't have used that word herself; heady, evocative, provocative, ecstatically pleasurable—that was what kissing Dominic was!

But had he lost all sense of reason?

It would seem that he must have done, she hazily acknowledged as she gasped her pleasure at his marauding mouth against her throat. Her neck arched as her eyes closed instinctively.

And suddenly she no longer cared, either, that after this they would probably never be able to face each other again without embarrassment and awkwardness.

Her father, a man who had loved life and had it taken from him at the young age of fifty-three, had always maintained that life was for living, that there should be no skirting around it in an effort of self-protection. Because of that philosophy he had lived every one of his years to the full before terminal illness had taken him from them. But he had died with all his family knowing that he hadn't left behind a life of unfulfilled wishes and 'if only's.

And she wasn't going to have any more misgivings about this time with Dominic, either. She would take what he offered, whatever it might be.

With a soft cry of compliance she moved her arms up about his neck as her body curved into his, loving every pleasurable sensation that action caused.

'Oh, Cathy,' Dominic groaned. 'Dear God, the warmth of you!'

Warmth didn't begin to describe the raging inferno that exploded between them, a fire that had her gasping with pleasure at the moist heat of Dominic's mouth on her breasts as she explored every hard inch of his body with hands that trembled in the shy compulsion. Lips that searched, hands that caressed, bodies that cried

out for a burning satisfaction neither of them
could deny.

And when that moment came it seemed to
last forever, and yet for the briefest, most
beautiful moment in time, suspended pleasure
that made them soar and peak before gently
falling back to earth with their bodies still
entwined.

Cathy stretched with the sensuousness of a cat,
cosily warm beneath the duvet despite her
nakedness.

Nakedness...

Her lips flew wide open as she realised from
the glowing ache she felt in her body that the
memories she had of last night were no dream,
that every ecstatically beautiful moment of it
had been a reality.

Dominic had made love to her, all night long,
with a gentle intensity that made her cheeks
blush and her breathing become raggedly
erratic.

She turned to him, quickly, eagerly, only to
find she was alone in the sofa-bed they had
made up for themselves some time in the night.
She frowned as she saw the sheet of stark white
paper, with Dominic's distinctive heading on
it, propped up against the pillow next to her
own.

Her hand shook as she reached for it and read the words, 'I'll be back as soon as I can,' signed with the unmistakable scrawl that was Dominic's name.

He had gone back to the car without waking her first...

CHAPTER SIX

The morning after the night before.

It had to be the worst experience in anyone's life. Especially when the man you had just shared the night before with disappeared the next morning before you were even awake.

It could have been the most ecstatic or miserable morning of Cathy's life. And there was no doubt in her mind which one it was for her.

A twenty-six-year-old virgin, seduced by a man it was—still—futile to love; there could be no doubt this was the worst moment of her life.

Dominic had been gentle with her, anticipating her every need for caution, initiating her into lovemaking with a tenderness that had made her cry and silently plead with him not to voice the stunned question in his eyes as he looked down at her so concernedly.

It had been a moment in time that had stood still, never ending, but seeming so quickly over, only to be claimed by singing emotions that had led them both to the edge of an ecstasy Cathy hadn't imagined existed.

And still that question had remained unanswered, for their bodies were entwined in a warmth that had needed no fuel to relight it moments, seconds later.

Dominic had proved a wonderful lover, a man completely unselfish in his lovemaking, his body a sculpture of hard planes and bronzed skin that had awakened a response within Cathy which still made her tremble with a yearning she now had to deny.

She stood anxiously at the window searching for some sign of Dominic's return as she watched the bleak snow-covered countryside before her.

How long had he been gone? The note had said he would be back as soon as he could; it gave no indication of what time he had set off.

He could already have been out there for hours, for all she knew; she had been so completely exhausted that nothing had disturbed her dreamless sleep, not even the removal of that heated body that had given her so much pleasure.

How long *had* he been gone?

A sob caught in her throat as she accepted the fact that he could be lying somewhere out there helpless in the snow right at this moment.

He had no right to just go off like that without telling her, even if they had agreed he should go this morning. It was thoughtless, arrogant—completely in character, in fact! She should really have realised he might do something like this.

Where *was* he?

How *dared* he?

God, by the time he got back—she refused to contemplate that it might be an *if* he got back—she was going to be ready to personally throttle him for causing her this anguish.

And, knowing Dominic as she did, he would probably wonder what all the fuss was about!

Damn the man, he——

All reproach, all anger left her as she saw his dear, familiar figure coming towards her in the snow. She let out a glad cry of relief as she turned and ran to the door.

He looked haggard, bowed, as she flung open the door to welcome him.

But her joy turned to amazement as she realised he wasn't alone. Clinging limply to his arm, almost too weak and weary to put one foot in front of the other, it seemed, was a young girl.

Cathy was just too stunned to move, and by the time she had forced some energy into her limbs the couple had reached the cottage door. And as they did so she realised it wasn't a child that clung to Dominic at all, but an exquisitely beautiful woman.

'What——?'

'I hope you've got the fire lit so that the two of us can thaw out,' Dominic rasped without preamble as he strode inside, the woman following in his wake giving Cathy a feeble smile as she entered the cottage.

Cathy followed them dazedly as Dominic went through to the lounge, arriving just in time to see him helping the exhausted woman on to the sofa. 'What——?'

'She's been in her car all night, somehow managing to keep warm by wrapping herself in a car blanket,' Dominic turned to her briefly to explain, his expression grim. 'She's lucky she didn't die of hypothermia.'

'Dominic!' Cathy scolded as the woman seemed to become even more pale—if that were possible; she looked exhausted with the cold and from the trek to the cottage.

He straightened, standing back, with his hands thrust into his trouser pockets. 'What on earth possessed you to be out on the road in that weather?' he snapped, his eyes narrowed.

Whatever conversation the two of them had had before they reached here, it obviously hadn't covered that subject, and, looking at the other woman as she reclined so exhaustedly on the sofa, Cathy didn't find that so difficult to understand.

'What on earth possessed *us* to be out on the road in that weather?' Cathy returned impatiently, going down on her haunches beside the woman, uncaring that she was probably bringing Dominic's wrath down on her own head now. After all, *she* was the reason they had been driving in this area at all. 'A hot drink would be the best thing, I think,' she told the other woman gently.

'Thank you.' The woman smiled weakly, her eyes the clear deep blue of pansies, the exquisitely lovely face framed by thick, dark hair that tucked neatly beneath her jawline.

And yet there was a vulnerability about her that seemed to owe nothing to the conditions under which she had been found, a purple bruising beneath her eyes that increased her fragility, a hollowness to the pale cheeks that spoke of deep unhappiness, hands that were far too slender moving restlessly at her sides.

'I don't even know your name,' Cathy spoke her thoughts out loud, all the time knowing that she knew much more about this woman than was perhaps wanted.

'Ann,' the woman supplied huskily. 'Ann Freeman.'

Cathy nodded as she straightened. 'Just rest, Ann, and I'll get you some tea.'

'Make mine a coffee,' Dominic rasped, his expression still distant.

Cathy gave him an impatient look as she left the room; he wasn't being very sympathetic to the other woman's plight. It couldn't have been easy sitting in a car all night wondering if you were going to see the morning. But then Dominic was probably exhausted himself, she excused with a slight blush to her cheeks; neither of them had slept much during the night, and then he had been for that long trudge in the snow this morning.

But he was a forbidding sight, standing so unyieldingly across the room as she came back with the tray of tea and coffee.

Ann sat up to take her cup, looking a little better now, the heat from the fire having put some colour back in her cheeks. But the haunted expression still remained in her eyes. 'If I could use the telephone——'

'There isn't one,' Cathy told her regretfully, instantly wishing she hadn't had to be so negative as the other woman paled again. She glanced with sympathy at the wedding band on the left hand. 'Your family will be worried about you.'

'Yes,' the other woman acknowledged distractedly, glancing out of the window at the heavy grey sky. 'I felt sure there would be a telephone here...'

Cathy shook her head. 'It's only a holiday cottage, you see.'

Ann turned back anxiously. 'Do you think we will be here long?'

'We both have other places to go too, you know,' Dominic rasped.

'Dominic!' Cathy turned to him in horrified outrage; what on earth was wrong with the man, that he should treat Ann in this way?

'No, no, it's all right,' Ann excused him tautly, giving Dominic a nervous glance. 'I'm being insensitive.'

'Not at all,' Cathy assured her, shooting Dominic another censorious glare—to which he appeared totally impervious as he met her gaze unflinchingly! 'We've had a lot more time to get used to the idea that until someone actually finds us here our friends and families are pretty much in the dark about our whereabouts.'

Dominic still looked at the other woman with narrowed eyes, his hands in his pockets pulling the material of his trousers tautly across his thighs. 'You still haven't explained what you were doing out in a snowstorm on Christmas Eve.'

Anne frowned at his persistence, her throat moving convulsively. 'I——'

'How about some breakfast?' Cathy interrupted brightly. 'We're pretty limited, I'm afraid.' Even more so now that there were three of them! 'But I'm sure I can rustle something up.'

'I'll help you——'

'No, stay where you are,' she cut in firmly as the other woman would have stood up. 'Dominic can help me,' she added firmly with a determined look in his direction, waiting pointedly beside the door for him to leave with her.

With a shrug of his shoulders he preceded her from the room, and Cathy waited only long enough for them to reach the relative privacy of the kitchen before turning on him.

'What on earth do you think you're doing?' she demanded, her eyes glowing with anger. 'The poor woman is half frozen to death, desperately worried about her family, and yet you're treating her like—like some sort of criminal!' she realised with a frown.

His expression was coldly remote. 'Why *would* a married woman be wandering about in a snowstorm on Christmas Eve?'

'I don't know,' Cathy dismissed impatiently. 'Any number of reasons, one would imagine. It's really none of our business, is it?'

He gave a terse acknowledgement of his head. 'I don't like mysteries.'

'Oh, for heaven's sake, Dominic!' She moved agitatedly about the kitchen, preparing them all some breakfast. 'Her reasons are probably as innocent as ours.'

His eyes narrowed, but for all that he was still unsmiling, Cathy could tell his mood had changed. 'Can you still believe that after last night?'

The flush in her cheeks burnt hotly. In truth, the night she had spent in his arms had been pushed to the back of her mind during the last fifteen minutes. How that was possible, even during that strange exchange with Ann Freeman, she didn't know! She had spent the night in this man's arms, and knew him as intimately as he undoubtedly knew her.

Not that it was *this* man in whose arms she had spent the night. Last night she had known a Dominic she had never seen before. And from the look of him now, from his coldness since his return, it didn't seem very likely she would ever see him again.

'Last night just—happened,' she said awkwardly, her face slightly averted.

'Did it?'

She looked up at him sharply, her cheeks still flushed. 'You surely don't think that I——'

His mouth twisted. 'You could hardly have arranged for the lousy weather that stranded us here.'

'Then what——'

He straightened. 'Forget it, Cathy,' he dismissed tersely. 'Let's all have that breakfast, then maybe we'll feel better.'

She had never known food improve *his* mood before, and this morning proved no exception. The three of them consumed the strange fare in silence, a thoughtful one on Ann's part, awkward on Cathy's, and coldly reserved on Dominic's. Cathy was relieved when it was over, even more so when Dominic tersely excused himself, muttering something about collecting firewood.

Ann looked slightly less fragile after eating and drinking something, insisting on helping this time as Cathy cleared away.

'I really am sorry to have just—landed myself on you in this way,' she grimaced, wiping the dishes as Cathy washed them.

'Don't be silly,' Cathy protested, knowing Dominic's terseness was what had prompted the apology. Really, his behaviour was disgraceful; the poor woman would probably have frozen to death if he hadn't found her when he had and brought her back here, and now he was treating her like some interloper! No wonder Ann felt uncomfortable! 'I'm just glad Dominic found you,' she added with sincerity.

'So am I,' Ann said ruefully. 'But I'm sure your husband—— '

'Oh, Dominic and I aren't married,' Cathy instantly denied. 'I'm his personal assistant. At least, I was,' she amended awkwardly, a blush rising to her cheeks as she realised she was babbling. 'I no longer work for Dominic, but until yesterday I was his PA,' she insisted firmly, knowing her explanation still left a lot of questions unanswered—such as what the two of them were doing together at all yesterday!

'I see.' The other woman nodded, obviously not 'seeing' at all. 'I'm sorry if my assumption embarrassed you.'

'Oh, it didn't,' Cathy dismissed with a sigh, knowing it would probably have angered Dominic into a quick denial if he had heard it. Married, indeed. He would have walked through a blizzard to get help for them first! 'And you mustn't mind Dominic,' she excused him lightly. 'This is an awful time for any of us to be stranded like this, and Dominic's temper is a little frayed.'

The woman's control, fragile at best, suddenly seemed to break, and she buried her face in her hands as she began to sob.

'Hey, come on,' Cathy cajoled, her arms going instinctively about the other woman's shoulders as she continued to cry. 'It can't be as bad as all that.'

'It's worse,' Ann choked. 'Oh, God, I've behaved so badly!'

Cathy patted her back soothingly. 'I can't believe you've done anything that serious——'

The other woman pulled back slightly. 'Walking out on my husband and children on Christmas Eve, having my two babies wake up this morning to find Mummy isn't there to celebrate with them—that isn't serious?' she challenged self-disgustedly.

Cathy swallowed hard, taken aback by the vehement outburst.

What on earth had possessed this woman to behave in such a way? Had it been out of defiance? Desperation? What?

Whatever the reason, Ann obviously bitterly regretted it. But it was too late to change things now, and to a child there could be no excuse for a parent's being missing on this morning of all mornings. And both women knew that as they stood in that cold, unwelcoming kitchen with the wind howling outside.

'I'm sure you had your reasons,' Cathy placated her unconvincingly, her mind buzzing with what those reasons could possibly be. Whatever they were, Ann seemed to have made the mad flight alone. Unless there had been someone else involved and his desertion was what had brought Ann to her senses. Too late, it would appear. But it was no good speculating on the whys and wherefores of the situation; it couldn't help or change anything.

'Yes, I had my reasons,' Ann acknowledged harshly. 'Somehow they no longer seem important.' She shook her head, her eyes brimful with fresh tears.

'Ann——'

'It doesn't help, you see.' She spoke almost to herself. 'Knowing the reasons doesn't help at all,' she choked.

'Ann, you——'

'Because all I can see, all I can imagine,' the other woman drew in a ragged breath, 'are the faces of my two little girls this morning as they bravely try to show their daddy they don't mind that I'm not there because they know his heart is breaking!'

A movement across the room caught Cathy's attention, and she looked up just in time to see Dominic staring at Ann with such a look of vehement dislike that it made her gasp out loud.

CHAPTER SEVEN

'KEEP your voice down, Dominic, she'll hear you,' Cathy hissed furiously.

'I don't give a damn whether she does or not,' Dominic rasped as he continued to pace restlessly up and down the kitchen.

With the thought of keeping the tearful Ann as far away from Dominic as possible, Cathy had persuaded the other woman she might feel a little better after a lie-down and possibly a sleep.

Ann did look exhausted, and Cathy was sure that tiredness was only adding to the other woman's already emotional state, but the suggestion had been made as much to get Ann away from Dominic's obvious fury as anything else.

The other woman was resting in the sitting-room now, as far as Cathy was aware, nevertheless, this was a small cottage, the walls quite thin, and Dominic was, typically, making no effort to lower his voice.

He was absolutely disgusted with what he had overheard of the other woman's story. In fact, Cathy had the distinct impression that if he had known of the circumstances of Ann's being stranded in the snow before bringing her back here he might have been sorely tempted to leave her in the snow to take her chances!

The fierceness of his reaction was completely unlike him. He was a gentle man given to few extremes of emotion, and his anger now was all the more awesome because of that.

'Do you have any idea how her children must be feeling right now?' His eyes glittered dark green with fury.

'I have a pretty good idea.' Cathy nodded heavily, thinking of those two tiny woebegone faces among the glitter that was Christmas. The children had to be relatively young; Ann couldn't be much older than her own twenty-six years.

'You can't have,' Dominic dismissed harshly, his face etched with tiredness and anger. 'Not really, not unless you've experienced that type of loss for yourself.'

And suddenly Cathy knew that Dominic had.

She knew that Dominic's parents had both died when he was eight, and from his reaction now she would say it was probably around Christmastime when it had happened. The circumstances of that loss weren't known to her, but she could see now that, whatever they were, it was this that had soured Christmas for him.

He had gone to live with a maiden aunt, but it didn't appear to have been a close relationship, and Cathy could imagine a little boy with curly dark hair and pain-filled green eyes hardening his heart to the world, but especially to Christmas. If what she suspected was true it was no wonder he had chosen to continue turning his back on Christmas even when he was an adult. And she had always assumed it was because he was too busy making his millions to bother with the occasion.

There were so many things, with hindsight, that she could have done to make it different for him, ways she could have slowly changed his disillusionment with Christmas if she had only known at least part of the reason behind it. But she had been too busy thinking of him in the terms of a 'bah, humbug' Scrooge that she hadn't taken the trouble to get to the bottom of *why* he was the way he was. And she loved him. How off-putting his attitude must have been all these years to people who only knew him as Dominic Reynolds, the businessman. She could have wept for him.

But, logically, she knew that wasn't going to solve anything now.

'Dominic, whatever Ann's reasons for doing what she did, we can't judge her on them,' she pointed out gently. 'We're all stuck here together until help comes, and we have to make the best of it,' she encouraged.

His mouth was tight. 'Then the quicker we get out of here, the better!'

If things had been fraught before, Cathy could see they were going to be virtually impossible now. She was going to have to act as a buffer between Dominic and Ann; heaven knew the poor woman was already suffering enough without Dominic's anger descending on her.

But that was much easier decided than accomplished. Ann was so lost in her own misery that for the most part Cathy was sure she didn't even notice Dominic's glowering behaviour on the occasions when they were all together—occasions which Cathy, through sheer desperation, kept to a minimum by whatever means she could! It was like walking through a minefield, expecting the explosion at any moment, but praying it wouldn't come. But Cathy knew it was only a matter of time before it did; Dominic wasn't known for his reticence.

After they had dined more frugally than ever that evening, on the food that had seemed so plentiful yesterday but which now seemed to be dwindling fast, Cathy surreptitiously watched Dominic as he sat and drank his way single-handedly through a bottle of wine as she tidied away the debris from their meal.

In spite of the fact that she knew he rarely touched alcohol, the wine didn't seem to be having any effect on him, it was true, but from the grim expression on his face he didn't look as if he intended stopping at the one bottle. And although Cathy had never seen Dominic drunk—in fact, she had more than once wished he would lighten up enough to show such a human weakness—she didn't think here and now, especially under the circumstances, would be a very good idea.

'Haven't you had enough?' she prompted lightly as, sure enough, he began to open a second bottle.

'Join me,' he invited abruptly, continuing to open the bottle.

'I don't think so.' She shook her head. 'And I don't think you should have any more, either,' she added softly.

His brows rose arrogantly. 'I'm not driving,' he derided.

Cathy drew in a controlling breath. 'Shouldn't we try and keep as much of the alcohol as we can, possibly for medicinal purposes if nothing else? After all, we don't have any idea how long we're going to be here.'

The thought of that was enough to make him pour out a glass of wine from the new bottle and drink it down in one swallow before pouring himself another glassful.

'Dominic!' She frowned her agitation with his behaviour.

He gave her a cynical smile. 'It is Christmas, Cathy,' he reminded mockingly.

'I had noticed.' They had come a long way from the joy she had found yesterday evening in his thoughtful gift of the tiny Christmas tree!

'Then you shouldn't begrudge me a little Christmas cheer.' He raised his glass in a toast before drinking some of the wine without even a grimace, despite the fact that she had never known him to drink red wine at all, and even white wine only in small quantities; he was going to be roaring drunk before too long. Just what they needed!

'A little!' she scorned, glaring at him accusingly.

His eyes narrowed to steely slits. 'I'm not drunk, if that's what you're implying.'

Not yet!

She gave an exasperated sigh. 'No one was suggesting you are——'

'Weren't they?' He stood up, instantly dwarfing the kitchen.

The reckless glint in his eyes made Cathy feel nervous. 'Ann is all alone in the sitting room——' She broke off abruptly, realising as she saw his eyes darken and his mouth firm that mentioning the other woman had not been the best of ideas at the moment. 'Dominic, we can't stay out here in the kitchen all evening when she's in the other room,' she reasoned exasperatedly.

'You may not be able to,' he acknowledged tautly. 'But, believe me, I have no trouble whatsoever in doing so.'

Cathy had already guessed that. Not that Ann was likely to say too much about his absence; she clearly considered Dominic's behaviour odd anyway, and would probably be relieved at the respite from the tension Dominic seemed to engender.

'Don't you think you're behaving a little childishly?'

'Childishly?' he repeated forcefully, his hands clenched at his sides. 'I don't even want to breathe the same air as that woman!'

'Dominic!' Cathy gasped disbelievingly, shaken by his vehemence.

'I've never been a hypocrite, Cathy,' he rasped. 'And I'm not about to start now. That woman goes against everything I believe in——'

'You don't know that——'

'I heard the same admission you did, Cathy,' he bit out harshly. 'The woman walked out on her family at Christmas.'

'That's none of our business.'

'Maybe not.' Dominic nodded tersely. 'But she was the one who chose to tell us.'

'She chose to tell *me*,' Cathy corrected pointedly. 'And then only because she was upset and needed to talk to someone.'

'And so she ought to be upset!'

Cathy looked at him appealingly. 'Dominic, she looks ill,' she reasoned softly. 'She doesn't need our passing judgement on her for something we really know nothing about.'

His eyes glittered with dislike. 'Well she isn't going to get my sympathy, if that's what you mean!'

'I just want you to be polite to her,' Cathy said exasperatedly. 'This situation is unpleasant enough without your treating Ann as if she had something contagious.'

Dominic's brows rose. 'You don't actually condone what she's done?'

'I don't *know* what she's done,' she sighed impatiently. 'Neither of us does.'

'We know enough to realise her children are without a mother today,' he said coldly. 'How would your two nephews feel if Penny had disappeared over Christmas without explanation?'

She thought of her two young nephews, past the age now of 'believing in Father Christmas', but still young enough to appreciate this special family time together; and they would hate it if Penny weren't with them.

'They would hate it,' she conceded. 'But they would accept it if they had to,' she said with certainty. 'Dominic, aren't you basing your re-action on your own experience——?' She broke off with a guilty gasp, realising she had spoken aloud the thoughts that had occurred to her after his earlier reaction. And from the thunderous expression on Dominic's face it was obvious he would rather she had kept those thoughts to herself!

He came a step closer to her, towering over her, despite her own considerable inches. 'What do you know of my "experience"?' His voice was silkily soft.

Cathy hadn't felt in the least threatened by Dominic in the past, no matter what the situation, and yet she felt slightly apprehensive of him now, having crossed, she knew, that unspoken barrier that had always existed between what he chose to let her know about him, and what he chose to keep to himself.

'Nothing, of course. But——'

'Nothing?' he repeated scornfully. 'Oh, come on, Cathy, I can't believe you held yourself aloof from the speculation that's gone on about me all these years!'

Cathy knew that he intended to wound, was deliberately doing so with the insult, but years of hiding her emotions came to her rescue and she didn't give him that satisfaction. She *had* held herself above gossip about him, but it had been because she loved him and refused to discuss him in that way, and not because of any lack of interest in him herself. She wanted to know all there was to know about him, but only if *he* chose to tell her.

'Speculation because of a mystique you've chosen to nurture,' she challenged defiantly, her head tipped back to meet his gaze with stready, unblinking eyes.

'Hell, woman, I didn't nurture it,' he flared furiously. 'I just don't see what right anyone has to stick their nose into my personal life!'

'Exactly,' she said with satisfaction.

Irritation scored his brow at her attitude. 'This isn't the same thing at all——'

'Of course it is,' she dismissed impatiently. 'The more of a mystery you make of your life, the more curious you make people to know about it; it's human nature.'

'Does this generalisation include you?' Dominic grated.

'I've already told you, no,' she snapped irritably.

'Never been curious, Cathy?' he taunted. 'Not even once?'

Her mouth firmed, deeply resenting having his anger turned on her in this way. 'Oh, I've been curious, Dominic,' she bit out tautly. 'But then, I'm as human as the next person.'

'Excluding me, of course,' he rasped scornfully. 'But I was very human last night, wasn't

I, Cathy?' he added self-derisively. 'So even I must have my moments of weakness.'

'We all have those, Dominic,' she said huskily, last night a vivid memory, all of it.

'That's my excuse—what was yours?' His expression was hard. 'Or were you just taking that curiosity you admitted to a step further?'

She saw her hand swing up in an arc of movements through an angry red haze, heard the cracking sound as her palm made contact with his cheek, her hand stinging from the contact, his cheek turning vividly red even as she continued to look coldly at him. 'I'm going into the other room with Ann,' she informed him distantly, turning away, not in the least surprised—or, at that moment, concerned—when he chose to remain in the kitchen with his wine for company.

He could drink every bottle of wine in the cottage for all she cared, could drink himself into unconsciousness—and she hoped that in the morning he had the biggest, most painful hangover of his life!

Ann was asleep in one of the armchairs when she entered the sitting-room, and didn't even stir as Cathy made her more comfortable, pulling across the other armchair to slide the other woman's legs up on to and covering her with a duvet. That only left the sofa-bed for herself and Dominic to sleep on, but the chances of Dominic actually wanting to sleep with her tonight were extremely remote, she felt sure.

How *could* he have made that cutting remark about last night, a night that had meant something to her even if it hadn't to him?

How could it *not* have meant anything to him?

He simply wasn't the type of man to go around making love to a woman on a whim, especially when the two of them had had such a close working relationship for so many years. She knew that he was upset with Ann, that he had drunk too much alcohol when he wasn't used to it, but his coldness towards her hurt none the less.

What did she know of his private life, anyway? It had always been work between them, always, but there were times when Dominic chose to be on his own, when he excluded her completely; what did she know of what he did during those times? One thing she did know: last night a man who had known exactly what he was doing had made love to her . . .

Quite how she managed to fall asleep on the sofa-bed, with her thoughts in such turmoil, she didn't know, but she woke slightly as she felt the duvet being placed comfortably about her and then the warmth of a hard body as it moved up close against her.

'We need the combined body warmth,' Dominic murmured in answer to her murmured protest.

She wanted to ask 'What about Ann's body warmth?', but the heat of his body made her feel so cosily comfortable that it was much easier to snuggle into that body warmth and drift back off to sleep. Even the smell of wine on warm breath didn't disturb her unduly; in fact it was rather pleasant as she turned to bury her face against the warmth of Dominic's naked chest.

'I'm not sure this was such a good idea,' he murmured gruffly.

Cathy snuggled even closer, her hands moving lightly across his back.

'Cathy——!' Dominic's strangulated groan was very telling, his body tense.

'Sleep, Dominic. I only want to sleep,' she protested in a drowsy voice.

'That's all I wanted to do when I came to bed, but hell, woman——!' He drew in a ragged breath, his arms tightening.

She was tired, so very tired. Lack of sleep last night, and the tension today, had made her so.

'Ann,' she reminded huskily.

He drew in a harsh breath. 'Go to sleep, damn it!' he rasped through a set jaw.

'I am, I am,' she muttered drowsily, relaxing against him completely.

'I wish I could say the same,' was his wry comment as she drifted off to sleep.

CHAPTER EIGHT

WAKING up with a feeling of complete dis-orientation was something Cathy was becoming used to. Or at least it should have been. Although this morning was somewhat different, an insistent—and persistent—noise, breaking through the warm mists of sleep she had been floating in.

'What the hell?'

Dominic's harsh exclamation so close to her banished any last remnants of sleep, and Cathy opened her eyes to find herself looking at his dishevelled state beside her on the sofa-bed as he jack-knifed into a sitting position.

Their puzzlement turned to surprise as they both became aware of the fact that the insistent noise that had awakened them both was a loud banging on the front door, accompanied by the occasional muffled shout.

It was at about this time that they both also realised Ann was no longer in the room.

Dominic was the first up off the bed, despite the fact that his reflexes had to have been dulled somewhat from the alcohol he had consumed the night before.

'What's the woman up to now?' he muttered as he hastily pulled on his clothes.

Cathy frowned as she stood up. 'Are you sure it is Ann?' The voice sounded distinctly masculine to her, even if it was muffled.

'Who else?' Dominic gave her a sharp look. 'It would be too damned much to hope that we're going to be rescued from this place!'

She hung back as he hurried from the room, knowing as she heard the deep tone of men's voices seconds later that they were indeed about to be rescued.

And she was drawn between the relief of that, of being able to let the family know she was well, and the knowledge that, once they had left this isolated little cottage, Dominic would make his excuses to leave as soon as he possibly could. Who knew when she would see him again after that?

But common sense had to prevail; they were getting low on food and fuel, and Ann—Ann! Dear God, where was she?

Her greetings were vague to the two policemen as they stood talking to Dominic in the hallway, and she hurried past them.

'Cathy?' Dominic's puzzled voice stopped her, obviously wondering why she wasn't as delighted as he was by the 'rescue'.

'Ann,' she reminded tautly, irritated that he could have forgotten the other woman.

'She can't be far away.' He shook his head. 'Try the kitchen.'

'This would be the Mrs Freeman we were just making enquiries about?' The younger of the two policemen frowned.

'Ann Freeman, yes.' Cathy nodded distantly; she couldn't hear any movements in the kitchen, and the cottage was too small for her not to be able to do so if Ann was in there. Surely the other woman wouldn't have left the cottage on her own? She surely couldn't have been so desperate to get back to her husband and children that she would have done something that silly?

'Her husband has been very concerned about her.' The older policeman shook his head.

'Indeed?' Dominic's sarcasm couldn't be concealed.

'Dominic!' Cathy glared warningly; whatever his personal opinion of Ann, he had no right to voice it in front of these two men.

'As I understand it,' Dominic continued scornfully, 'Mrs Freeman had chosen to leave her family even before she got caught in the storm.'

Cathy knew that it was his absolute fury at the woman's apparent desertion of her husband and children that was making him behave in his way, and yet at the same time she could sense the other men's disapproval of his obvious censorship.

'Domestic crises are very common this time of the year,' the younger man told him firmly. 'Statistics show——'

'Statistics don't help the people left behind,' Dominic rasped unrelentingly.

'Mrs Freeman, sir,' the older policeman said firmly. 'If we could just locate her——?'

'Of course,' Cathy cut in briskly, taking charge of the situation, as she could see Dominic's disgust with Ann had still got the better of him. 'She must be in here—oh, my God!' she gasped with a groan as she saw Ann lying on the kitchen floor, apparently unconscious.

She could only stand helplessly by as the two policemen sprang into action, attempting to revive the unconscious woman.

Cathy was racked by terrible feelings of guilt that she had been sleeping while this poor woman had been lying on the cold, lino-covered floor, and she could see that the unexpectedness of their discovery had finally shaken Dominic out of his unrelenting mood as he went down on his haunches beside the policeman while Ann slowly seemed to be coming round.

It soon became obvious that Ann wasn't quite sure what had happened to her, either, although it was obvious by the expression on the policemen's faces that they were as concerned by the faint as she was, deciding she needed to be taken to hospital straight away.

After that it was a blur of movement as the two policemen and Dominic helped Ann out to the Range Rover that had been their form of transport up to the cottage. Cathy asked to sit in the back with the other woman as they drove as quickly as they could to the nearest hospital so that Ann's condition could be checked out, in spite of her protests that she was fine now.

'Are we going to be all right now?' Ann's voice was husky as she held on tightly to Cathy's hand.

'Of course,' Cathy reassured her lightly, knowing that a lot of Ann's nervousness must be concerning her family's reaction to her when they saw her again. 'Your husband has been very worried about you,' she added encouragingly. After all, if the husband was worried about Ann then he couldn't be too angry at her disappearance, and that had to be good news.

Tears instantly filled the big blue eyes. 'Poor Paul. And the girls,' she choked. 'Oh, God, my poor little girls.' Sobs racked the slender body.

The policeman sitting in the passenger seat turned to give Cathy a censorious glare for obviously upsetting Ann before murmuring words of comfort to the stricken woman.

She hadn't meant to make Ann cry, only to reassure her, surely they could see that? Although, after Dominic's behaviour, perhaps they couldn't!

Dominic sat beside her in the Range Rover, his face stony. He hadn't spoken a word since they had found Ann. Not that he ever was a great conversationalist, but this silence wasn't like that.

His only sign of emotion was a frown as they passed his car still nose-first in the snowdrift, although other traffic was now moving slowly along the cleared road.

Yes, the roads were now clear enough to travel along with care, but Cathy suddenly realised that Dominic didn't have anything to travel along *in*, not until his car had been pulled out of the snowdrift and the damage corrected.

She gave him a sideways glance; did he realise that he was effectively stranded in Devon for the moment? Maybe that was part of the reason he suddenly looked so chillingly angry!

'I think it would be best if you and Miss Gilbert let a doctor take a look at you,' the older policeman told Dominic as they pulled up outside the hospital.

'That won't be necessary,' Dominic answered haughtily.

'Nevertheless, I think it's a sensible precaution, Mr Reynolds,' the other man insisted firmly.

Dominic's mouth twisted. 'Hypothermia didn't have a chance to set in, if that's what you're worried about.'

Was it Cathy's imagination, or did both the other men keep their eyes discreetly diverted after that derisive jibe?

'It isn't, sir,' the older man replied smoothly. 'But that would appear to be a nasty bump you received to your head at the time of your accident, and I believe it might be sensible to have it looked at, at least.'

Cathy knew by the man's manner that Dominic's attitude had rubbed them up the wrong way, but that the policeman was still intent on doing his duty couldn't be denied. And he had put that last statement in such a way that Dominic was going to look more than a little silly if he still refused the hospital checkup.

It was instinctive, despite the fact that he had got himself into this awkward position by his own stubbornness, to leap to his defence. 'I'd like to go in with Ann, anyway,' she said lightly. 'Just to make sure everything is all right.'

'In that case it appears we have no choice.' Dominic nodded abrupt agreement.

'Thank you.' Ann squeezed Cathy's hand gratefully.

'We radioed ahead.' The young policeman got out of the vehicle. 'So both families will have been informed of your safety.'

So much had been going on since their 'rescue' that it had completely slipped Cathy's mind that Penny and Simon would still be worried about her, and the relief now that she knew that at least the police had thought to let them know was immense. Poor Penny and Simon, what a Christmas they must have had, worrying about them, and Jade and David too. She felt even worse about making this an upsetting time for them.

The accident department of this large hospital was as officious as most, although slightly less bustling than usual, perhaps because of the time of year. Nevertheless, they were dealt with speedily and efficiently, and Cathy was quickly passed as fit, although Dominic had to have an X-ray on his head, and the doctor insisted on carrying out several tests on Ann.

There was a protest from Ann when it came to this, at which Dominic gave a disdainful look down his arrogant nose, and which Cathy chose to ignore; after the upsetting couple of days the other woman had had, she was entitled to have minor hysterics if she wanted to.

When a worried-looking man of about thirty came rushing through the door about half an hour after their arrival, Cathy had no doubt as to his identity. Her certainty that this must be Paul Freeman was confirmed as he spoke to the receptionist and she pointed in their direction as she answered him.

He was quite a handsome man, tall, and as dark as his wife, although his good looks were marred by his worried frown as he hurried over to them.

'Ann——?'

'She's fine,' Cathy instantly assured him, standing up to smile at him. 'She's with the doctor now, and——'

'Doctor?' he echoed worriedly, glancing towards the closed doors that led to the examination-rooms. 'Is she ill? They didn't say anything about that when——'

'She isn't ill,' Cathy soothed him, giving Dominic an angry frown for not helping her reassure this stricken man. Couldn't he see that Paul Freeman was worried out of his mind about his wife? Surely he could forget his personal prejudice against Ann for the moment. 'But we did find her unconscious——'

'She *has* been injured——' The man's panic returned.

'Just a slight fall,' Dominic cut in firmly, also standing up. 'It isn't anything serious,' he added with slight impatience. 'Why don't you sit down? I'm sure she won't be long now.'

Paul Freeman didn't so much sit down as fall down, landing heavily in a chair as his legs no longer seemed capable of holding him, a dazed look on his face. 'I don't understand any of this,' he buried his face in his hands. 'Ann loves me and the kids, I'm sure of it,' he told them fiercely, as if daring them to deny it was true. 'What would make her do something like this?' He looked at Cathy appealingly.

She swallowed hard. 'I don't——'

'I know things are difficult at the moment,' he continued as if she hadn't answered him, 'that we haven't had an easy time of it lately, but——'

'I'm sure your wife will explain everything to you once the doctor has finished with her,' Dominic calmed him irritably.

The panic in Paul Freeman's face didn't lessen. 'Oh, God, I hope she's all right. Nothing else matters as long as she's all right.'

'Of course she is.' Cathy patted his arm awkwardly. 'We've all been examined. It's just routine after an experience like this one.'

He looked hopeful. 'Is it?'

'The police insisted on it,' Dominic agreed dourly, obviously still displeased at their request.

Paul gave a self-derisive grimace. 'I somehow thought I would just be able to pick Ann up, take her home, and forget any of this had ever happened.'

Cathy watched the surprise, and then curiosity, flicker across Dominic's face. Obviously this hadn't been the reaction he had expected from Ann's husband at all.

'Excuse me for saying so,' he said quietly, 'but your wife told us she had left you when she got caught in the storm.'

Paul bristled resentfully at the reminder. 'She had her reasons, I'm sure of it.'

Just as Cathy was sure he was right in his earlier claim that Ann loved him and their children. Whatever Ann's reasons for leaving them at this time, it hadn't been because of any lack of love on her part. Or Paul's, by the look of him.

Dominic continued to look at him searchingly for several minutes, before shrugging his shoulders dismissively. 'There's a machine just outside in the corridor where we can get some drinks. Why don't we go and get some coffee while we're waiting for the doctor to come back?'

Cathy watched the two men as they left the room, looking through the money in their pockets for the right change for the machine. She was just relieved that the meeting had passed by without incident. The way Dominic had backed down was too puzzling to even think about just now. She had half expected him to advise the other man to cast Ann aside and tell her never to darken his door again!

But her relief turned to anxiety again as the two men didn't return straight away, and she chewed worriedly on her bottom lip, afraid that Dominic had taken this time alone with the other man to voice his opinion, and half expecting him to come back with another bruise on his face, this time inflicted by a punch. Not that Paul Freeman looked any more powerful than Dominic, but he would have pure anger on his side to spur him on!

Finally it was the nurse's returning that necessitated Cathy's going in search of the two men. They stood in the corridor quietly talking, obviously with no intention of a fight breaking out. She wondered briefly what they could have been talking about—on the surface they seemed to have little in common—and then she remembered the reason she was here.

'The nurse says you can go in and see Ann now,' she told Paul softly.

Relief brightened his face, and then he frowned. 'See her? You mean they haven't let her go yet?' Panic strained his voice. 'What——?'

'She's probably just resting,' Dominic calmed him. 'She did faint, remember.'

The other man didn't look any less worried as he hurried back to the waiting-room, his movements uncoordinated in his distress.

'Poor devil,' Dominic muttered grimly.

Cathy gave him a sharp look. Why did he have to be so damned hard and cynical all the time? Couldn't he see that Paul Freeman didn't care why his wife had left him the way that she had, that he was just grateful to have found her safe and relatively well again? Love like that was incomprehensible to Dominic, she knew.

'We may as well have that coffee now,' he said drily. 'I have a feeling we've still got a long wait ahead of us.'

Cathy could cheerfully have hit him for his obvious cynicism. But what good would it do? Nothing she did or said at this late stage was likely to change Dominic's opinion of love and emotion, not if their having made love so beautifully hadn't reached him.

Paul was missing when they returned to the waiting-room, but the nurse stood waiting for them. 'You're both free to go now.' She smiled brightly, a tiny redhead with a pretty freckled face. 'Your X-rays were fine, Mr Reynolds, although the doctor advises you take it easy for a few days yet,' she added briskly.

Dominic frowned at the air of authority in this tiny woman. 'And what, exactly, does that mean?'

She shook her head. 'I think he would prefer if you didn't travel back to London for the time being.'

'But——'

'Mr Reynolds has no intention of travelling back to London immediately,' Cathy cut in firmly. 'He will be staying at my sister's home for the next few days.'

'Oh, I will, will I?' Dominic taunted once the nurse had left to return to her duties.

'Yes, you will,' Cathy answered challengingly. 'Use your common sense, Dominic,' she continued fiercely. 'You've been involved in an accident, you have a nasty bruise on your head, and you've spent the last few days in a freezing cold cottage; you need the rest badly!'

He raised dark brows. 'Was I arguing?' he mocked softly.

'You need to just take things easy for a few days, and you'll be able to do that at—— What?' She had suddenly realised what he had said.

He shrugged. 'I'm quite willing to accept that it would be more sensible to take advantage of your brother-in-law's invitation in the circumstances. And no, I'm not in more pain or feeling more exhausted than I've been telling you,' he drawled at her searching look. 'I just realise it would be the best thing to do.'

She could never remember that making any difference to him before. Dominic had always been a law unto himself, whether he was right or wrong. Maybe that bump on the head had affected him more than he realised!

Whatever the reason for his agreeing to stay at Penny and Simon's after all, it didn't really matter; all that was important was that he *had* agreed.

And now, far from parting today and never seeing each other again, as she had been expecting would happen, they were going to spend the rest of the holiday together. It had to be the longest goodbye. Oh, what sweet torture!

Although from the way Dominic was looking at her now you would never know the change that had occurred in their relationship during the last couple of days, never realise the rapture she had known in his arms. But she had felt the quickening of his body as he lay beside her the night before, knew that he hadn't felt that desire for one night only, that last night he had fought against wanting her.

'Good,' she answered him inadequately, disturbed by her own thoughts.

He chuckled wryly. 'You're very inarticulate all of a sudden!'

She pulled a face. 'Having you agree to something without argument would have that effect on an angel!' she defended.

His mouth twisted. 'And we both know you're too spirited to be that!'

'You——'

They both turned as the swing doors into the examination-rooms swung open with a bang and Paul Freeman hurried into the room, a Paul Freeman who looked dazed and yet jubilant at the same time.

Cathy stood up, unsure of what could possibly be wrong. Ann had seemed fine a few minutes ago—a little shaky, perhaps, but otherwise quite well in the circumstances. She sensed Dominic moving to stand at her side.

'Paul, what——?'

'She's pregnant!' he announced to no one in particular, almost seeming to be talking to himself. 'Ann is pregnant!' Excitement entered his voice, his eyes starting to glow as he looked at them. 'The timing is lousy, which is why Ann panicked and ran the way that she did, but we're expecting a baby in seven months' time!'

CHAPTER NINE

'THAT was rather unexpected, wasn't it?' Cathy remarked casually.

Dominic had been strangely quiet since Paul Freeman had made his excited announcement.

The two of them were once again alone in the waiting-room. Simon was expected to pick them up at any moment, and Paul had returned to his wife's side.

Cathy had been in to see Ann briefly before they took her down to the ward they had decided to admit her to just so that they could keep an eye on her for a few days and make sure there were no complications.

When Cathy had entered the examination room, the other woman had certainly looked happier, clinging on to her husband's hand as if she might never let go.

Ann gave a sheepish grimace. 'I just didn't know which way to turn once my pregnancy was confirmed, you see. Paul doesn't have a job at the moment because the firm he was working for made him redundant several weeks ago. Christmas had been a nightmare to organise as it was, without my dropping this extra burden on Paul; I stupidly thought he and the children would be better off without me.' She gave a wan smile.

'Never,' Paul denied fiercely. 'We'll manage, love, you'll see.'

'Things do have way of working out,' Cathy put in quietly, her heart going out to the other couple, her reassurances sounding weak and meaningless; but what else could she say?

'That's what I said,' Paul nodded. 'Darling, we made this baby together, out of love, just as we did Chrissie and Rachel.'

Cathy had blinked back the tears at the simple sincerity of that statement. What did it really matter that Ann and Paul were struggling at the moment? They had each other, and a love strong enough to get them through it. Nothing else really mattered.

Although she doubted Dominic saw it that way. And she had a feeling something else about the situation was bothering him. 'The possiblity of *my* being pregnant is extremely remote,' she told him distantly. 'So I wouldn't worry about it if I were you!'

He looked at her blankly for several minutes, then a rather stunned expression came over his face, as if the idea hadn't even occurred to him before now.

Then what had he been looking so distracted and pensive about?

'I wasn't worried about it.' He frowned.

'But you are now,' she realised with a sigh as he still looked stunned.

His mouth firmed. 'Not for the reason you are obviously supposing. But, as you said,' he added abruptly, 'the possibility is very remote.'

Nevertheless, it *was* a possibility, and one that filled her with an aching longing, re-kindling that impossible dream she had once had of a dark-haired baby in her arms with green eyes. Dominic's child. But it would be silly to let her imagination run away with her again, although she couldn't help feeling en-vious of Ann.

'You——'

'Cathy!' came a glad cry from the doorway, causing them both to turn sharply, just in time to see Penny hurrying across the room towards them. 'Thank heavens you're safe!' she choked as she reached Cathy and the two of them fell into each other's arms.

Cathy returned the hug, tears flooding her eyes at the relief of seeing her sister again. Now that they were together again she had to admit to herself that there had been a couple of times during the last few days when she had wondered if it would ever happen.

'We've been so worried about you.' Penny was crying unashamedly as she stood back to look at her. She was a blonde, like Cathy, but there the similarity ended, Penny being 'short and cuddly', as Simon liked to say affectionately. 'The boys have refused to have Christmas until you can be with us.' She laughed shakily.

'Oh, no,' Cathy groaned emotionally. 'The little darlings!'

'Don't let them hear you call them that.' Penny grimaced. 'Although, to be honest, the two of them only realised last year that there's no such thing as Father Christmas!'

'Where's Simon?' Cathy frowned, unable to believe her brother-in-law would have let Penny drive all this way on her own.

'Parking the car,' her sister supplied ruefully. 'I couldn't wait that long to come in and make sure you really were all right.'

'I don't——' She suddenly became aware of Dominic standing just behind them, having stood up as soon as Penny entered the room. 'Penny, I don't think you've met Dominic Reynolds.'

Her sister's eyes widened on him curiously, and Cathy bit her lip to stop herself from smiling, able to read almost exactly what Penny must be thinking: this gorgeous man was the one Cathy had claimed was a tyrant and a despot!

'How nice to meet you at last,' Penny said warmly, holding out her hand, recovering well from the surprise she had just received. 'I had

no idea—— You see, when the police informed
us that two women, one of them Cathy, and a
man, had been rescued from a remote cottage,
we assumed—at least, I did—that it was Cathy
and another couple. Well, I know how
stubborn Cathy can be,' she added with af-
fection. 'And so I was sure she wouldn't have
accepted your offer to drive her here, Mr
Reynolds——'

'Dominic,' he put in quietly.

'Dominic,' she repeated, a little too coyly for
Cathy's comfort. 'But I was sure Cathy would
be driving down alone, that she must have
taken refuge with the other couple. I had no
idea,' she repeated brightly, obviously thrilled
by the way things had turned out. 'You really
must accept our invitation to stay now,
Dominic.'

'I——'

'Cathy!' A jubilant Simon came bouncing
into the room, trudging snow from outside
across the floor despite having wiped his shoes
as he entered, the receptionist frowning at him
as he did so, although with his usual innocence
Simon remained unaware of the fact. 'Thank
God you're all right!' He gave Cathy a bear-
hug. 'You had us worried, pumpkin,' he told
her softly.

'I hope I haven't ruined your Christmas,' she said gruffly, all this emotion starting to make her defences crumble.

'Of course you haven't.' His eyes twinkled merrily. 'We can have an even better Christmas once we get you home; we have so much more to celebrate and be grateful for now.'

'Simon, this is Dominic Reynolds,' Penny informed her husband pointedly.

He turned to the other man with narrowed eyes, assessing him at a glance. 'Good to see you.' He held out his hand, obviously liking the other man. 'I had no idea——'

'We've already been through that bit once, darling,' Penny cut in affectionately. 'What say we load the luggage into the car and be on our way? We can talk on the journey, and the quicker we get back, the sooner we can reassure the others.'

Simon grinned at the other man as he picked up one of the suitcases. 'I hope Cathy hasn't given you too much trouble,' he teased, quirking a mocking brow at her.

She gave him a playful punch on the arm as they went outside.

'Not too much, no,' Dominic drawled, helping Simon put their things into the car. 'Although you're right about Cathy's stubbornness, Penny. I hadn't realised until recently just how stubborn she can be.'

Cathy glared at him, receiving an innocently questioning look back. As if he didn't know exactly what he was doing! 'I took lessons from an expert,' she returned with saccharine sweetness.

'Really?' He arched dark brows. 'I can't think who!'

'Can't you?' she returned drily, knowing from the look that passed between Penny and Simon that they were enjoying the verbal exchange, probably reading a lot more into it than there actually was. Or ever could be—despite the intimacy they had shared the last two days.

'I'm really sorry we've upset the boys' Christmas in this way.' She frowned, wanting to change the subject, take the focus off Dominic and herself, although she knew there would be questions from her sister later.

'Are you kidding?' Simon, firmly ensconced behind the wheel of the car, turned to grin at her. Dominic was sitting at his side at Penny's insistence that he would have more room there, and the two women were in the back of the vehicle. 'They think it's great that they still have Christmas to come while everyone else's is over!'

'I might have known,' she said indulgently, shaking her head.

Penny kept trying to attract her attention on the drive to the school that the other couple owned and ran, and Cathy knew her sister had to be dying of curiosity about the time she and Dominic had spent alone at the cottage. Well, she would just have to remain curious, even once they had chance to talk privately; there was no way Cathy could tell her sister just how close she and Dominic had become at the cottage!

Her sister gave up trying to catch her gaze, a frustrated look on her face, when it became obvious Cathy wasn't going to be drawn. The two men talked softly in the front of the car, and as Cathy listened to the steady tone of their voices she fell asleep.

The school, an ex-cottage-hospital that had been converted for the purpose, was strangely deserted, with the pupils at home enjoying their festive holidays, and yet the big old house that was Penny's and Simon's home looked beautiful with its blanket of snow in the garden and on the roof of the house itself. Cathy felt a flow of warmth as they all got out of the car.

'Anything to avoid spending Christmas with me, I see,' drawled a mocking voice.

Cathy spun around with a glad cry, launching herself into David's arms.

David was Simon's younger brother by a few years, and they both had those beautiful dark blue eyes, were both tall, but David's hair was much thicker and darker than Simon's, and the pain David had known at the death of his wife several years ago had etched marks in the handsome face that shouldn't have been there in a man so young. This was to have been the first Christmas they had all spent together for a very long time, David having chosen to distance himself from the family, and anything else that reminded him of losing Sara, since she had died. But all that had changed now, and Cathy could see the happiness shining in his eyes. She couldn't have been more happy for him herself.

'As you can see,' she laughed up at him, 'I'm not pleased to see you!'

He grinned down at her, his arms still about her. 'Oh, yes, I can definitely see that.'

'Where have you hidden Jade?' She looked around questioningly.

'She's taken the terrible twosome for a walk in the snow to wear off some of the excess energy they've been storing up the last few days.' He grimaced, his eyes widening as he looked past her and saw Dominic, his arm tightening about her shoulders as he faced the other man. 'You decided to come down after all, then?' His eyes were narrowed challengingly.

'If I'm not intruding,' Dominic nodded, giving away nothing of his own thoughts from his expression.

'Of course you aren't,' Penny took over briskly. 'We've already been through this conversation twice, David, once with me and once with Simon.' She frowned at him reprovingly.

'Sorry!' David held up his hand defensively before holding it out to Dominic. 'Reynolds.'

'Kendrick.' He returned the gesture coldly.

'David and Dominic,' Penny insisted, a little crossly. 'Now, let's all go into the house and stop freezing out here!'

David's arm about her shoulders made it impossible for Cathy to do anything other than go into the house at his side, leaving Dominic and Simon to bring in the luggage, Penny directing them which bedrooms to take it up to.

'Well?' David prompted softly as they entered the warmth of the lounge.

'Hm?' She looked up at him with questioning innocence, shrugging off her coat to stand in front of the fire. The house was filled with the aroma of a turkey roasting; dear Penny, she had even saved the Christmas lunch until she could be with them!

David gave a rueful smile. 'Not going to tell me, hm?'

She held her hands out to the warmth of the fire. 'There's nothing to tell.'

He winced pointedly. 'You make a terrible liar, Cathy.'

She returned his gaze steadily. 'Do I?'

'Jade will want to know all the wicked details,' he warned with relish.

'*Jade* might get to hear all the details.' She deliberately omitted the word 'wicked'.

'She'll tell me,' David challenged teasingly.

'Not if I ask her not to,' Cathy answered with certainty.

David grimaced. 'True,' he sighed. 'This "old girls" brigade is a bit unfair to us poor males. I don't suppose I could persuade it out of you?' he cajoled.

She smiled at his deceptive 'little boy' air. 'I don't suppose you could.'

He pursed his lips thoughtfully. 'I seem to remember you were always very ticklish...!'

'No, David.' She backed away from him as he advanced on her threateningly. 'That wouldn't be fair!' she squeaked as he began to tickle her, squirming away from him.

'Men and women never play fair,' he grinned as she choked with laughter. 'Now, do tell,' he encouraged conspiratorially.

'No!' She fought ineffectually at his tormenting hands.

'Come on, Cathy,' he persisted mercilessly. 'I want to know what—oh, hello, Dominic.' He glanced past her to the doorway. 'Just bringing a little masculine pressure to bear,' he explained in a mocking voice.

Cathy had spun around as soon as Dominic's name was mentioned, moving awkwardly away from David as Dominic watched them with narrowed green eyes. She hadn't done anything wrong, and yet the way he was looking at them made her feel somehow guilty!

'Indeed?' Dominic moved further into the room. 'Concerning what?'

Cathy could feel the tension between the two men, and she concentrated on smoothing her trouser-leg as a way of avoiding looking at either of them. They were grown men; whatever problem there was between them, they could work it out for themselves. She didn't need any more tension of her own.

David grinned mischievously. 'Concerning the two of you alone in that cottage for two days and two nights,' he challenged blatantly, making Cathy gasp.

Dominic didn't even glance in her direction, holding the other man's gaze. 'We were only alone for one of those days and nights,' he rasped. 'And we were hardly there by choice!'

'Oh, I realise that,' taunted David, unabashed. 'But once you *were* there...'

Dominic did give Cathy a sharp look at that, although the expression on her face must have told him all he needed to know about her own reticence concerning their time at the cottage.

He turned back to the other man. 'Once we were there,' he told David coldly, 'we were too busy worrying about being rescued to think of anything else.'

'All the time?' the other man derided. 'That sounds decidedly single-minded to me.'

'I am single-minded,' Dominic said curtly, obviously seething with anger beneath the surface, his eyes glittering angrily.

'Hm, so you are.' David looked disappointed. 'I don't suppose—ah, I think I hear Jade now.' His face lit up at the thought of the woman he loved, the front door having banged shut, to be followed by the murmur of voices. 'I'll go and tell her you're here.' He strode quickly out of the room, obviously eager to be with Jade again.

Cathy gazed after him wistfully, envious of the love David and Jade had found in each other. If only things could have worked out for Dominic and herself.

'Jade,' Dominic echoed softly. 'I don't think I know her, do I?'

Cathy shrugged. 'Possibly not. There's really no reason why you should, although I would say she's the best friend I have.'

His mouth tightened. 'I've always been interested in your friends, Cathy.'

That was news to her, but there was really no point in dwelling on the past, or indeed on the last couple of days. It was all over, and all she had to do now was get through this last time together as best she could.

'That wasn't meant as any sort of criticism,' she sighed.

'It sounded as if it was,' he bit out.

'Well, it wasn't,' she added irritably, the sound of voices coming nearer now. 'Jade and David will be getting married soon,' she supplied vaguely, eager to see her friend once again.

'*What?*'

She gave Dominic a startled glance. What on earth was so disturbing about Jade and David getting married?

And Dominic did look disturbed.

CHAPTER TEN

'WHAT an absolutely fascinating man,' Jade remarked thoughtfully.

Fascinating? Maybe Dominic was that, but he was also puzzlingly enigmatic, if not downright unfathomable. From the way he had reacted when Cathy had told him about Jade and David, one would have thought she had just announced that David was to marry some two-headed monster instead of the lovely green-eyed, auburn-haired woman who was Jade.

Her own conversation with Dominic had been put aside in the excitement of seeing her friend again, and Cathy had put the incident from her mind as they all went in to have lunch.

It was only later that afternoon, when Jade had offered to help her unpack, that the conversation had come back to her. Not that the time-lapse helped at all; she still didn't understand what had disturbed Dominic so much about the announcement.

And she was no more sure she could confide in Jade about the last few days than she could earlier in David. It was all so raw and painful still that she didn't really want to talk about it. To anyone.

157

Her mouth twisted. 'That's one way of putting it.'

Jade raised questioning brows at her derision. 'David obviously admires him very much.'

Yes, he obviously did hold the other man in great respect, but that wasn't the same as liking him. 'As a businessman I'm sure he does, yes,' she nodded.

Her friend shrugged. 'From the little he's said about him the last few days, I don't think he knows a lot more about him than the business side. He gave me the impression that there weren't many people who do.'

Cathy's face shadowed over as she paused in the act of putting silky underwear into a drawer. Penny and Simon's house was big enough to accommodate any number of guests in comfort.

Until the last few days she hadn't known enough about Dominic's past life to be of any personal help to him, and now it was too late, their relationship having changed too much for her ever to be able to approach the subject of his past with any degree of detachment. And emotional pleadings just wouldn't reach him, she knew that only too well.

'No.' She sighed acknowledgement of that sad fact, returning to her unpacking.

'But you love him.'

Cathy gave her friend a startled look, not because it wasn't perfectly obvious to anyone who really knew her how she felt about Dominic, but because it wasn't like Jade to be so blunt. Shy and retiring Jade never intruded, had always been the best friend anyone could ever hope for.

Jade made a face at her obvious surprise. 'David is already a terrible influence on me.'

She smiled. 'Oh, I wouldn't go that far.'

'Neither would I, really.' Her friend gave a coy smile. 'But I only had to take one look at you and Dominic together,' she sobered, 'to realise how you felt about him.'

Cathy sighed at the truth of that. 'And how do you think he feels about me?' she prompted, without any illusions.

Jade gave a rueful shrug. 'It's very difficult to tell. He certainly doesn't give much away by his behaviour.'

'Exactly!' She sat down heavily on the bed, giving up all pretence of unpacking; they both knew it had only been an excuse in front of the others so that they could slip away for a quiet chat.

Jade sat down beside her. 'What *did* happen during the last couple of days?' she encouraged gently.

'Everything! And nothing,' Cathy amended shakily, her eyes brimful with tears as she looked up at her friend. 'Does that make any sense to you?' Her cheeks were fiery red with what she knew she had revealed to Jade.

'I think so,' her friend said slowly, her face full of compassion.

'But it's no good,' Cathy choked. 'Whatever happened—happened, as far as Dominic is concerned. And now it's over.'

'Are you sure?'

'Oh, yes,' Cathy dismissed self-derisively.

'It's difficult with a man like that to tell what he feels,' Jade frowned.

Cathy shook her head. 'Believe me, that— part of our relationship is over. And as I no longer work for him, either—— '

'That's a new development, isn't it?' Her friend looked concerned.

'Very,' she confirmed drily. 'Although it's since before this Christmas fiasco.'

Jade looked more puzzled than ever. 'Then why did he——?'

'Don't ask.' Cathy grimaced. 'I haven't been able to work out for myself yet why he should choose to drive me down here, let alone feel I can explain it to anyone else!'

'Hm. It's very curious, though,' Jade said with slow thoughtfulness.

'Don't read too much into it,' Cathy dismissed disgustedly. 'Dominic is merely a law unto himself and, if he chooses to do some- thing, he doesn't believe anyone should question it.'

'I can tell that,' her friend said, still very thoughtful. 'But it is—curious.'

She shook her head. 'I wouldn't dwell on it too much. Over the years I've come to realise Dominic is simply unfathomable.' She stood up briskly. 'Now, let's finish off this unpacking before David gets too lonely and sends out a search-party,' she attempted to tease. 'I get the feeling he suffers from withdrawal symptoms if you're away from him for too long!'

Jade blushed prettily. 'The feeling is mutual,' she admitted shyly. 'But are you really sure you're going to be all right?' She looked at Cathy searchingly.

'No,' she admitted in all honesty. 'But I'll cope.'

'Sure?'

'No,' she admitted again. 'But I don't really have any choice other than to at least try.'

'Just call on me if you need help,' Jade offered warmly. 'And David will leap to the rescue if he feels you need it, I'm sure.'

Cathy raised her eyes heavenwards. 'I have a feeling that fiancé of yours would like to cause trouble, given the chance!'

'But David is extremely fond of you,' her friend protested.

'As I am of him,' she smiled. 'But he's always been a terrible tease!'

'Yes,' Jade agreed with a light laugh. 'But I will try to make him behave, I promise.'

Cathy grimaced. 'From what I know of David I have a feeling that *trying* to make him behave just won't be enough.'

She knew she was right when they rejoined the others in the lounge. David was sitting in an armchair beside Dominic's, and was looking so obviously frustrated that both women knew he had been pumping the other man for information while they were out of the room—and obviously getting absolutely nowhere! It would have been quite funny if Cathy couldn't tell by the coldness of Dominic's expression that he didn't in the least appreciate the intrusion.

Cathy and Jade looked at each other knowingly, but it was left to the huskily spoken Jade to try and pour oil on troubled waters as she joined the two men, sitting on the carpet at David's feet to rest back against his knees.

Jade might be quiet and shy, but she also had the ability to put people at their ease, and Cathy could see Dominic begin to thaw after only a few minutes in her company. She herself joined her two nephews on the floor as they revelled in playing with the toys they had finally unwrapped a short time ago.

Cathy turned her full attention on them. 'I must say I think you're very good to have waited until today to open your presents.'

Peter, the oldest by only a year, grinned up at her. 'It wouldn't have been Christmas this year without you.'

Considering how long it had been since she had actually been free to spend Christmas with them, Cathy was touched by her nephew's remark, and she swallowed hard, frowning as she glanced up and saw the strange look that had come over Dominic's face. It was an unreadable look, almost too fleeting to have been there at all, and yet she knew she hadn't imagined that almost—lost—yes, lost look on Dominic's face for the briefest moment.

It had been as if he had come up against something he didn't understand, something he couldn't control, at least. And that was almost impossible to believe.

Although, on reflection, maybe it wasn't so unbelievable after all. A family would be difficult for him to cope with or understand. A family that had remained close despite prolonged absences must be incomprehensible to him.

But her family liked Dominic, she could tell that from their open warmth towards him. Which was possibly just as much of a puzzle to him! Poor Dominic.

'Toys have changed a lot since we were their age,' Simon was saying to him, watching his sons indulgently as they set up an elaborate space-station and its accompanying space vessels.

Cathy watched Dominic's reaction warily; if she was right in her suspicions he would have been about the boys' age when his own life had changed so drastically. From the little he had said in the past about the maiden aunt who had brought him up after his parents' death, there had been little cheer in her house, either at Christmas or any other time of the year.

But she needn't have been worried; he just looked slightly bemused as he too watched the boys playing with their mound of toys. 'They certainly have,' he murmured appreciatively.

'Come and help us,' James invited a little shyly, still slightly in awe of Dominic. Although Cathy knew from experience that that wasn't likely to last very long.

Dominic looked slightly uncomfortable at suddenly being the focus of attention, although to Cathy's surprise he didn't refuse the invitation but came down awkwardly on the carpeted floor beside them.

'As long as your Aunt Cathy stays too,' he said lightly.

She had no intention of going anywhere, although his request for her company surprised her. Although, on reflection, he probably thought she would help act as a buffer between him and the boys, knowing it would look rude to refuse to play with his host's children. But to Cathy's knowledge he had never got down on the floor and played with any children before. To her knowledge he had never come into such close *contact* with any before!

'Very domesticated,' David drawled mockingly as she helped Penny with the tea later.

Cathy turned to give him a derisive smile. 'I can be as domesticated as the next woman.'

'Oh, I didn't mean you,' he taunted. 'When I left the living-room just now Dominic was stretched out on the floor with Peter, setting up his train-set.'

'And why shouldn't he?' she defended, a flush to her cheeks.

David's mouth twitched. 'When was the last time you saw Dominic playing with a train-set?'

'David——'

'Brought tears to your eyes, didn't it?' He quirked mocking brows. 'Very touching.'

'David!' she sighed, glancing across at Penny as she briefly returned to the kitchen after taking some of the food out into the dining-room.

'It was like trying to get blood out of a stone earlier,' he mused thoughtfully. 'Dominic was quite the gentleman.'

'Some men are,' she said pointedly.

David grinned. 'I find all this too interesting to be a gentleman about it.'

'You——'

'Come on, you two,' Penny scolded, unable to avoid hearing their conversation. 'Everyone else is waiting to eat. You can talk later, if you must,' she added in a disgruntled voice, implying that she found their behaviour very rude.

The opportunity for David to talk to Cathy alone again didn't come later. He and Jade wandered off alone somewhere, for which Cathy was very grateful.

Dominic had continued to act out of character all evening, pleasant but very quiet. The two of them were suddenly left alone for a while when Penny and Simon went upstairs to say goodnight to the boys at the end of a very full day.

'You have a very nice family,' Dominic told her softly.

She felt a little uncomfortable, being alone with him after all that had gone before. 'I think so,' she replied awkwardly.

Dominic stood up to move about the room with restless movements. 'I want——' He broke off, frowning, suddenly looking unsure of himself.

'Yes?' Cathy prompted sharply, slightly unnerved by his manner; she had never seen him quite like this before.

He drew in a deep breath. 'I want to—thank you,' he said tightly.

She looked at him dazedly. *Thank* her? But for what?

'For today.' He couldn't quite meet her gaze as he explained himself, seeming embarrassed by his own words. 'For letting me share it with you,' he added stiffly as she continued to stare at him.

Her brow cleared a little. 'Penny and Simon——'

'Were kind enough to invite me initially.' He nodded abruptly. 'But I'm thanking *you* for letting me share your family Christmas.'

'I don't know what you mean.' She shook her head dismissively.

He gave a rueful smile. 'I think you do. A little.'

His reaction to Ann. The realisation she had come to at that reaction. But there was more. So much more.

'Today meant a lot to me,' he told her softly. 'More than I can say.'

Oh, God, she didn't like to see him like this; it wasn't the Dominic she knew. Even his arrogance would have been welcome at that moment.

He laughed softly at her expression, pulling her gently to her feet. 'Don't look so worried, Cathy, I haven't "gone over the edge"!'

She wasn't so sure. She hardly recognised this man. Not that she didn't like him—she just didn't know him very well! But then, she had a feeling that Dominic didn't either, which was probably adding to his own strange mood.

'You're a very special lady, Cathy,' he murmured huskily, his gaze searching her face. 'I always thought so, but I hadn't realised just how special you are. But then, in a way, I don't think I wanted to.' He frowned.

'Dominic——'

'I don't think I can really talk about this any more just now, Cathy,' he said without any of his usual cold aggression. 'I have a lot of things to think about, a lot of prejudices to—— Well, I can't explain it very well just now.' He cradled each side of her face with warm hands. 'My world is shaking on its foundations, Cathy,' he explained huskily. 'And it isn't a feeling I'm comfortable with.'

Tears filled the dark, smoky grey depths of her eyes. 'I wish I could do something to help you,' she choked, knowing even as she said it that she couldn't.

'You already have.' He rested his forehead on hers, looking deeply into her eyes. 'More than I can tell you.'

'Dominic?' She looked up at him concernedly.

'I told you,' he chided softly. 'Don't worry.'

'But——'

'Don't—worry.' He tapped her lightly on the nose.

'But I don't like to see you unhappy.' She shook her head.

'I know, and that's one of the things I have to think about.' He smiled gently to take any sting out of his words. 'But I'm less unhappy now than I have been for a very long time,' he reassured her.

He was different, she could see that, although it was difficult to pin-point in quite what way. Perhaps there was a vulnerability about him that had never been there before. If that was so, she was sure that was what he was having the problem with. Vulnerability was not an emotion she would ever have associated with Dominic, and she was sure it was one he had eradicated from his life at an early age.

She looked at him searchingly, but he just continued to smile at her in that gentle way, giving nothing more of his emotions away.

'You're leaving, aren't you?' she realised suddenly, slightly panicked at the thought.

'In the morning,' he confirmed softly. 'You know me so well,' he murmured appreciatively. 'I wonder why I never realised that before.'

She didn't know him that well, really, although she had to admit she probably knew him better than most people—but then, that wasn't saying much! But she had at least tried to understand him even if she hadn't completely succeeded. Maybe that was the difference; most people didn't even try.

But he was leaving, she had guessed that from the things he had said, the way he had looked. Was he going out of her life forever, or would she see him again?

'I'll be in touch,' he promised, reading the question in her eyes.

It wasn't much to cling on to, but it was more than he had ever given her before. And she dared not push him for any more of an answer than that; he was too unpredictable at the moment.

'Today was—nice,' she told him huskily.

Dominic nodded. 'Today was very nice. But it all only adds to my confusion.'

Confused? Dominic? It wasn't an emotion she would once have thought him capable of.

He gave a wry smile. 'Incredible, isn't it?' he acknowledged self-derisively.

'I didn't——'

'I did.' He put silencing fingertips on her lips, laughing softly. ' "How are the mighty fallen", hm?' he mused. 'But I have a feeling it was long overdue.'

Cathy looked at him searchingly; this really was a Dominic she had never seen before.

'I——'

'Oops, are we interrupting something?' an overly innocent-looking David stood in the doorway, an embarrassed Jade at his side.

Dominic turned slowly, keeping one arm about Cathy's shoulders. 'Not at all,' he answered smoothly for both of them.

'Sure?' David persisted mischievously—to Jade's increasing discomfort.

'Very,' Dominic drawled ruefully, not at all perturbed by the other man's behaviour.

'That's OK, then,' David answered lightly, although it was obvious by the slight irritation in his eyes that he would have liked more of a reaction. 'Jade and I were just about to have a drink. Care to join us?' He came into the room.

It wasn't the easiest of times, with David doing his best to be annoying, and Dominic fending him off with lazy amusement, but the rest of the evening did pass, and all too quickly for Cathy when she was so aware of Dominic leaving in the morning. It was bittersweet torment being with him like this, and in the end she couldn't stand it any more and excused herself on the pretext of being tired; she had never felt less tired in her life!

She hadn't been in her room long, only time enough to have showered and put on a nightgown, when there was a gentle knock on her door. She didn't feel in the mood for sharing any more confidences with Jade tonight, much as she loved her.

It was Dominic who stood outside her bedroom doorway.

Cathy just blinked at him, too surprised to speak, her peach-coloured nightgown clinging to her lovingly in the lamp's glow.

'I wanted to say my goodbye to you in private,' he told her huskily. 'The ever-watchful David will be observing us tomorrow,' he explained drily.

She grimaced. 'I'm sorry about that; it's his idea of humour.'

Dominic nodded. 'I got to know him reasonably well a couple of years ago. Cathy,' he added seriously, 'there's something else I need to say to you before I go.'

She stiffened defensively. 'Yes?'

He glanced around at their lack of privacy with him still standing out in the hallway. 'Could I come inside for a few minutes?'

Cathy frowned; what could they possibly have left to say to one another? And then she realised.

'Yes, come in,' she invited abruptly, preceding him into the room, turning sharply as she heard him close the door. 'I told you the possibility of my being pregnant is very remote, and I meant it, so I don't want you to think about it any more,' she bit out with hurt anger. 'I wouldn't bother you with it even if—even if something did happen!' Her head went back defensively.

'You damn well would!' His eyes glittered angrily.

'No, I——'

'Cathy, I didn't come here to argue with you,' he cut in disgustedly.

'Then what do you want?' she challenged.

'To thank you!' His voice was raised almost to a shout.

She frowned. 'For what?'

'For the greatest gift any woman can ever give a man!' he returned hardly. 'Oh, God,' he groaned, shaking his head, 'this conversation wasn't supposed to be like this. Cathy, we haven't really talked about the other night, except in the vaguest of terms, but I——'

'Don't,' she choked, her cheeks fiery red. 'I can't talk about that.'

'Can't, or won't?' he prompted softly, crossing the room to her side. 'Cathy, I couldn't believe it when——'

'I said *don't*!' she ordered shakily, turning away from him.

'Cathy——'

'Please don't,' she quivered against him as he turned her towards him. 'Please!'

He looked at her searchingly, her eyes swimming with unshed tears, her mouth trembling. 'Dear lord, you are the most incredibly beautiful woman! Cathy...'

She wanted him so badly, knew the need was echoed in his own eyes as their lips met and fused, hurting her in their fierceness at first, and then becoming more sensuously demanding as passion claimed them both.

Her nightgown rustled silkily to the floor at her feet, Dominic's clothed body abrasive against hers. He shrugged out of his own clothes with impatient movements, all the time their lips still fused in melting passion.

And then there were no more barriers between them, burning flesh melding into burning flesh, everything but each other forgotten as they were pounded with the tides of passion.

Cathy lay replete in his arms, her head on the warmth of his shoulder. Their lovemaking had been even better than before, more desperate on her part, more warm and giving on Dominic's.

This unexpected closeness had been such a surprise that Cathy couldn't help cherishing the memory of it.

'I shouldn't have done that,' Dominic finally said grimly.

She couldn't look up at him, had already known that what had just happened changed nothing between them.

He looked down at her, raising her chin with gentle fingers. 'I wasn't being fair to you.' He grimaced with self-disgust.

Tears filled her eyes. 'It didn't matter.'

'Of course it mattered.' He kissed her brow. 'I'm sorry, Cathy,' he sighed heavily. 'Really sorry.'

'But it was what I wanted too,' she protested awkwardly.

He shook his head, pulling gently away from her to get out of bed. 'I have to go.' He pulled on his clothes.

'Dominic——'

'Try not to think too badly of me.' He paused at the door.

Think too badly of him? She loved him, damn it! But if he couldn't see that—or didn't *want* to see it—there was nothing she could do now to convince him to stay.

Tears squeezed through her closed lids as she heard him leave, and her body soon ached from the shuddering sobs she was determined to suppress.

When she came downstairs in the morning it was to find he had already left.

CHAPTER ELEVEN

'HEARD from him yet?'

Cathy gave David a reproving look. 'This is supposed to be a party, David.'

'I know that,' he derided. 'Jade and I are the ones giving it!'

'Then as host you should be on your best behaviour,' she scolded.

'I merely made a polite enquiry of one of my guests,' he claimed indignantly.

Only they both knew it hadn't just been a polite enquiry.

It had been five days since she had gone downstairs to find Dominic had left her sister's house, and as far as she knew none of them had seen or heard from him since.

As David very well knew!

Cathy hadn't particularly wanted to come to this New Year's Eve party of David and Jade's, but Jade had so much wanted her to come, and as it was the first joint function the other couple had hosted, and as she knew how nervous her friend was about it, she hadn't liked to let her down.

But David's flat was crowded and noisy, and she couldn't help wishing she hadn't come, despite the fact that she knew most of the people here. She had escaped to the kitchen a few minutes ago, but she should have known David wouldn't let her get away with that.

'No,' she answered wearily. 'I haven't heard from Dominic.'

David shook his head. 'I don't understand it.'

'I do,' she sighed. 'Only too well!'

'I doubt it, Cathy,' David denied gently, still frowning.

Dominic's behaviour was only what she had expected; she shouldn't have been hurt by it. And yet she was. She had been expecting too much, she knew that, and yet a tiny part of her had continued to hope.

'Oh, but I do,' she said dully, turning away so that David shouldn't see her tears. She had cried a lot during the last five days. It didn't do any good, she knew that only too well, and yet she couldn't seem to help herself.

'Cathy.' David spoke softly behind her. 'The night before Dominic left Penny's and Simon's he and I had—a long conversation.'

She spun around at that, a frown on her face. 'But you couldn't have done! I mean——' She broke off, a blush rising to her cheeks. 'He was with me that night,' she finished quietly.

David nodded, as if he had already known that. 'But not all of it.'

Her cheeks were still fiery red. 'But——'

'Dominic didn't go to bed at all that night, Cathy,' David told her gently. 'He and I sat up drinking whisky and talking all night.'

'Dominic doesn't drink,' she protested, more for something to say than anything else; Dominic had done nothing *but* drink while they were at the cottage. But she just couldn't imagine what these two totally different men could have found to talk about all that time.

'He doesn't usually talk, either,' David's lightly teasing comment seemed to echo her own thoughts. 'But I can assure you that on that night he did both.'

'Oh.' What else could she say? She hadn't had any idea that the two men had sat up together that night...

'I would have thought——' David shook his head, frowning again.

'Yes?' she prompted absently.

He shrugged. 'Well, Dominic didn't give me the impression he intended just disappearing out of your life. He was confused, yes, needed time to sort out some things in his life, but I still had the impression——'

'Yes?' she prompted impatiently as he slowed down again.

'I invited him here this evening, by the way,' David sighed. 'Sent him an invitation through the post. Not that he replied, but I somehow thought he might—— Oh well,' he sighed again.

Cathy drew in a deep, shuddering breath. 'David, do you think I should go and see him?'
'Yes.'

Her eyes widened at his certainty. 'Yes?' she echoed hesitantly.

'Yes,' David repeated firmly. 'If the man is so confused that he still hasn't contacted you then he needs a push in the right direction.'

'What is the right direction?' Cathy sighed.

'You are,' he told her forcefully. 'I know it, Dominic knows it, *you* know it. Don't just stand back and let it slip through your fingers,' he added persuasively.

'We can't all be as single-minded as you,' she protested, knowing his pursuit of Jade had been merciless.

'Yes, you can,' he said without hesitation. 'Dominic isn't an easy man to understand, but I think I came a little closer to it that night we sat and talked.'

'Drinking buddies,' she derided.

He shook his head reprovingly at her levity. 'Dominic needs you, Cathy.'

'Dominic doesn't need——' She broke off the scornful protest at the look in David's eyes. 'I don't understand.' She looked confused.

'Need is sometimes harder to admit than love,' he said quietly. 'And when you feel both of them for the same person it can be almost impossible. Dominic is a man who has lived too long alone without either emotion; it must be almost killing to admit to feeling both. Even to himself.'

Cathy wanted to deny that Dominic could feel either, but she was too afraid to, in case David should agree with her! If she left the conversation like that, there was always a chance David was right.

'I don't suppose it would do any harm if I went to his apartment and wished him a happy New Year,' she said as casually as she could.

'I don't suppose it would,' David agreed, a knowing twinkle in his eyes as he followed her out of the room and into the hallway. 'And, while you're there, tell him the man he sent to me is working out just fine.'

'Man?' she frowned her puzzlement. 'What man?'

'Paul Freeman,' he supplied briskly, signalling to Jade to join them so that she could say goodbye. 'I own a printing company in his area,' he explained as he helped her on with her wrap, smiling warmly at Jade as she joined them. 'It was easy enough to find a job for a qualified man like Freeman once Dominic had explained the situation to me.'

Cathy had wondered about the Freemans often the last few days; she felt a tremendous warmth that between them these two powerful men in the business world had taken the time and trouble to think of them too.

'Cathy is going to see Dominic to wish him a happy New Year from all of us,' David explained lightly to Jade, his arm about her shoulders. 'I'd offer you some coal to take for "first footing",' he teased Cathy. 'But this is a centrally heated flat. Take some champagne instead.' He picked up a bottle that had been cooling on the drinks trolley. 'Tell him it was from us. And I hope you both enjoy it,' he added conspiratorially.

'Good luck.' Jade kissed her warmly on the cheek.

Good luck. The words echoed around her head again and again on the taxi drive over to Dominic's apartment.

What if he deliberately hadn't gone to David's tonight because he had known she would be there? What if he didn't want to see her? What if——?

Oh, damn the 'what if's! Anything had to be better than sitting in her apartment waiting for a telephone call that never came. At least after this visit she would *know*. Besides, she wanted to thank him for helping the Freemans. The fact that he had gone to that much trouble had to prove something—if only that he could see and accept Ann's predicament.

The huge oak door to his apartment looked even more forbidding than usual, and yet it wasn't that long ago that Cathy had felt no qualms whatsoever about being at his apartment.

She was shaking as she waited for a reaction to her ring on the doorbell, her heart leaping nervously as she heard some movement inside.

Her first thought as he opened the door was how magnificent he looked. Dominic was always ruggedly handsome, but in a dark dinner suit and snowy white shirt he was devastating.

'You're going out,' she blurted out in realisation; why else would he be dressed in this way?

His eyes glowed darkly green as he took in her own appearance in the clinging black gown and grey wrap-around.

'David and Jade sent me over with this.' She held up the champagne bottle, becoming flustered when he made no response to her first statement, and talking too fast in her agitation. 'As you didn't make it to their party,' she added lamely.

Dominic still looked at her with those dark, glowing eyes. 'I was just on my way over there.' His voice was husky.

'Oh!' She swallowed hard.

'To see you,' he added softly.

'Oh!' She sounded even more squeakily surprised the second time she made the exclamation.

'How have you been?' He looked at her searchingly.

'Fine.' She nodded; anyone could see she hadn't been sleeping well, that her eyes were dark, and her cheeks pale.

'I haven't,' he told her quietly.

Cathy looked at him with wide eyes; he looked as fit and healthy as she had ever seen him, and there was a new air about him, a sense of anticipation she had never seen before.

'Come inside.' He gently took hold of her arm and guided her into the entrance hall, closing the door behind them. 'I have some things I want—need to tell you,' he said as soon as they reached the austerely masculine living-room decorated in its beiges and browns. 'And then I want to ask you something.'

'If it's about a baby——'

'Will you stop going on about that, woman?' he scolded exasperatedly.

'But there definitely isn't one,' she felt compelled to make clear.

He drew in a ragged breath. 'OK, there isn't one. But whether there were or not has nothing to do with what I want to say to you.'

Cathy sat down abruptly in one of the spacious armchairs, dropping her wrap back against the leather.

'It's at times like this that I wish I smoked,' Dominic said grimly, shrugging resignedly before sighing heavily. 'To start with, the "S" of my middle name stands for Stanton. It was my mother's maiden name,' he explained gruffly. 'I stopped using anything but the initial on the day my mother walked out on my father and me one Christmas and the two of them were killed in a car accident when he tried to bring her back.'

The part about his mother having left them, particularly at that time of year, was what she had already suspected, although she hadn't realised the 'S' in his name stood for his mother's maiden name. That explained a lot in itself.

But she said nothing herself, knowing it was a time for Dominic to talk, not her.

'I was brought up by my aunt, my father's sister,' he said harshly. 'A cheerless woman who believed in making sure I knew exactly what a burden I was to her, even though she considered it her "duty" to at least supply me with the basics of life.' The last was stated without emotion. 'It was because of that attitude that I swore I would never be dependent on anyone else for money ever again.'

She had known a demon drove him, but she hadn't realised what it was.

'I hadn't realised—hadn't realised,' he started again, drawing in a deep controlling breath, 'quite how much I had let my past influence me until Ann came to the cottage that day and all my bitterness returned.'

Cathy wanted to tell him she knew what he had done for the other couple, but the time for that would come later. Dominic still needed to talk.

'Against Ann, this time,' he continued, running a hand through the dark thickness of his hair. 'Good God, the woman was desperate, at the end of her tether; no wonder she ran away. How the hell do I know my mother didn't go through a similar crisis? Even if she didn't, an eight-year-old isn't of any age to judge what was right or wrong. My father loved her enough to want to try to bring her back to us, and how do I know he hadn't succeeded and they were on their way back when the accident happened? I was so wrong about Ann; I could have been wrong about my mother too.'

He *had* been doing a lot of thinking the last week. But he looked more at peace because of it. That spark of hope she had retained the last few days began to flower again.

'I'd like to give her the benefit of the doubt, anyway,' he said quietly. 'Once I'd accepted that, it wasn't difficult to realise the mess I've made of my own life, all the things I've missed out on because of prejudices I don't even know if I have the right to feel.' He shrugged ruefully, as if he were finally shrugging off the past. 'Are you able to give me the benefit of the doubt?' He looked at Cathy hopefully.

Her heart leapt. 'In what way?'

Dominic shook his head. 'Women have been a non-event for most of my life, and for the past five years a *complete* non-event,' he grimaced. 'It was only when I faced the prospect of Christmas without you that I realised why that was.'

'Christmas without me?' Cathy repeated dazedly, vaguely recalling that strange look on his face that day Peter had made a similar comment.

'Cathy, I haven't needed any other women in my life since you came into it because you fulfilled every need I had at the time,' he said self-derisively. 'And when I thought you were rushing down to Devon to spend Christmas with David I have to admit you raised a few needs I never knew I had. A few emotions too.'

She swallowed hard. 'Christmas with David?' she prompted for something to say, trembling at the hopes—and dreams—his words had resurrected.

Dominic gave her an indulgent smile. 'You forgot to mention Jade or their engagement when you said David was at Penny's and Simon's.'

Her eyes widened. 'I did?'

'Mm,' he confirmed ruefully. 'It was bad enough that you no longer worked for me, but you seemed to be leaving to go to another man, too. I'd never felt jealousy before, but I definitely felt it then. I don't even know what my intentions were when I offered to drive you to Penny's and Simon's; I just knew I couldn't let you go without some sort of fight.'

'Why?' She was almost afraid to ask the question, but there could be no more pretence between them now.

'I could prevaricate and deceive us both again, but I need you too badly to do that. I love you too much, too.' He came down on his haunches beside her chair. 'I swore after I lost my parents that I would never love anyone again, but God, Cathy, the thought of life without you fills me with despair. Even more so since I've known the complete warmth of you.' He clasped her hand in his. 'I've dared to hope this last week, Cathy...'

There was no arrogance about him, only a silent pleading. 'I've loved you for five years, Dominic,' she told him steadily.

'Then why——?'

'Why leave you?' she finished with a soft sigh. 'Because I finally decided that loving you so futilely was destroying me.'

'Oh, God,' he groaned, briefly closing his eyes. 'I've only known a week of that uncertainty, and it's been self-inflicted because of all the other things I had to sort out in my mind; I don't know how you could have stood it.'

'I didn't have a choice,' she pointed out gently.

'And now?' He looked at her searchingly.

She moistened her lips. 'That's up to you.'

'We could use David's champagne to toast our future. That's if you'll marry me?'

He was still so vulnerable, was going to need a lot of loving. But no one could love him more than she did; no one ever would.

'That sounds like a wonderful idea,' she told him huskily.

He pulled her sharply into his arms, groaning into her hair, as if he hadn't known what to expect from her. 'I've been so afraid . . .' he admitted shakily. 'Needed you so much . . . Oh, God, Cathy, I love you!'

A miracle. They really were possible.

'What does it feel like to be becoming a godfather again?' Cathy teased Dominic lightly as the two of them lingered over Sunday breakfast.

A year had passed since that snowbound Christmas, eleven months since they had been married in the same church as Jade and David had a week earlier, and today was the christening of Jade and David's daughter, Lia Sara. Only three months ago they had been godparents to the Freemans' son.

'Daunting,' her husband replied ruefully. 'How does it feel, becoming a godmother again?' he returned teasingly.

'Daunting,' she laughingly echoed his reply.

The last year had seen a lot of changes in Dominic: he was softer, gentler, and there wasn't a day went by when she needed to doubt his love. It hadn't all been easy, but then she hadn't expected it to be, and the reward of being loved by Dominic and loving him in return had more than made up for any awkward moments they might have had.

'But not as daunting as the prospect of becoming parents ourselves,' she added softly.

Dominic shrugged. 'I'm sure we'll cope if the time ever comes—Cathy?' He looked closely at her suddenly glowing face.

She got up to come around the table to hug him from behind. 'I've been trying to find the right moment to tell you——'

'The right moment?' He pulled her down on to his knee, his eyes glowing his pleasure. 'I can't believe it! Are *you* pleased?' he suddenly faltered.

She looked up at him unblinkingly. 'Ecstatic!' Their dark-haired, green-eyed baby! Dominic's baby.

'You've given me so much——'

'We've given *each other* so much,' she corrected firmly, her fingertips on his lips. 'And now we're going to have a child to love and share, too.'

'Heaven!' He buried his face in her neck.

Yes, heaven.

Harlequin ◆ *Presents*®

Coming Next Month

Available in January wherever paperback books are sold, or through
Harlequin Reader Service:

In the U.S.
901 Fuhrmann Blvd.
P.O. Box 1397
Buffalo, N.Y. 14240-1397

In Canada
P.O. Box 603
Fort Erie, Ontario
L2A 5X3

Take 4 bestselling love stories FREE

Plus get a FREE surprise gift!

Harlequin Superromance®

THEY'RE A BREED APART

The men and women of the Canadian prairies are slow to give their friendship or their love. On the prairies, such gifts can never be recalled. Friendships between families last for generations. And love, once lit, burns hot and pure and bright for a lifetime.

In honor of this special breed of men and women, Harlequin Superromance® presents:

SAGEBRUSH AND SUNSHINE
(Available in October)

and

MAGIC AND MOONBEAMS
(Available in December)

two books by Margot Dalton, featuring the Lyndons and the Burmans, prairie families joined for generations by friendship, then nearly torn apart by love.

Look for SUNSHINE in October and MOONBEAMS in December, coming to you from Harlequin.

MAG-C1R

Harlequin romances are now available in stores at these convenient times each month.

Harlequin Presents
Harlequin American Romance
Harlequin Historical
Harlequin Intrigue

These series will be in stores on the 4th of every month.

Harlequin Romance
Harlequin Temptation
Harlequin Superromance
Harlequin Regency Romance

New titles for these series will be in stores on the 16th of every month.

We hope this new schedule is convenient for you. With only two trips each month to your local bookseller, you will always be sure not to miss any of your favorite authors!

Happy reading!

Please note there may be slight variations in on-sale dates in your area due to differences in shipping and handling.

HDATES